The Ginger Bread Man

The Ginger Bread Man
By Dominic R. Villari

Published by
Figment Press
www.figmentpress.com

Copyright © 2008 by Dominic R. Villari

ISBN: 978-0-9814940-1-2

About the Ginger Bread Man

The Ginger Bread Man is the story of a young man named Jacob's journey of self-transformation from mediocrity to magic. After leaving an unfulfilling office job, a seemingly chance meeting with a Baker sets his life on a new course. Through the guidance and tutelage of this mysterious yet dedicated man, Jacob learns the simplicity and enchantment of baking. Along the way he finds love, meets new people and even invents a new type of gingerbread cookie. Through baking, Jacob discovers magic in his everyday life.

About the Author

Dominic R. Villari was born in Riverside, New Jersey in 1971. He studied communications and multimedia at Rider College and Boston University. In these formidable years he was heavily influenced by the writing of South American magical realists such as Gabriel Garcia Marquez and Jorge Borges. After earning a masters degree, Dominic spent several years as an instructional designer. He has also worked as a graphic designer and interactive developer. Throughout his eclectic career and interests he has always remained a storyteller. After specializing in non-fiction writing for several years, in 2007 Dominic returned to the magical realist genre with his new novel the Ginger Bread Man.

1.

"What's the worst that could happen?" He would lose his job. He would have no income. He might lose his circle of friends. Most of them revolved around work. He might lose himself. He might have to admit the last ten years of his life meant little. He might realize he'd wasted the last few years of his life on insignificant goals.

He swept the question aside and went back to a report he needed to finish. Jacob read through the last few lines. He found it impossible to convert the blur of words into sentences. Jacob shook his head back and forth in an effort to rattle his attention back. He took a deep breath and began to type: What's the worst that could happen?

Jacob looked at his surroundings and felt his heart sink, pressing on his diaphragm. He winced to avoid a scream. Everything was the same as it had been the day he started. The colors were different and the computer was newer but it was all still the same.

"What's the worst that could happen?" Jacob could find himself sitting in the same chair contemplating the same thought ten years from now. He might be making more money but would still be insignificant. That was the worst that could happen.

Jacob pushed back his chair and stood up. He picked up the green coffee mug he'd gotten three years earlier as a pollyanna gift. He put on his jacket. Jacob started for the door and was gripped by a burst of fear.

"What's the worst that could happen?" By now the question seemed like an old friend. He set the coffee mug back down and walked to the door. Once outside he began to run.

Jacob didn't stop running until he reached the train. Even on the train he never actually stopped moving – pacing through car after car until he reached the front of the train. When the train reached his stop Jacob stepped out into the sun and his heart immediately rose in his chest.

Jacob ran away from the train station and through the center of town. He ran past the post office and past the furniture store. He ran past the bakery, where the baker was out front sweeping. "Run, run as fast as you can," chucked the baker as he swept.

Jacob slowed to a walk and looked back. "Can't catch you," said the baker. Jacob stopped and turned completely around.

"Don't remember that old story, eh?" asked the baker. "An old woman baked a gingerbread man. But when she opened the oven, he popped out and ran away."

"Like I'm running," suggested Jacob tentatively.

"That's right," said the baker smiling and shaking his head. "You're the Gingerbread Man."

"I am the Gingerbread Man," replied Jacob. He was grinning ear to ear for the first time in many days. He turned and continued to run.

"Watch out for the fox!" called the baker after him.

Jacob ran until he reached his house. He was still smiling as he unlocked the door and stepped inside. The light beneath the phone was blinking. As a reflex he picked up the phone and dialed the number for voice mail. "Jacob...where the hell did you go this afternoon..." Jacob quickly pressed the delete key and put the phone back in its cradle.

"What's the worst that could happen?" The question popped back into his mind as he flopped down on the couch. Three days out with no call and they would terminate him. He would have to live off his savings for a while. He might have to borrow some money from his parents.

Jacob decided he could always take a job in a retail store. That would pay some bills and stretch his savings. He could sell off some of the items in the house he didn't use anymore. He could trade in his car for something with a much lower payment. He didn't need all those cable channels. Jacob paused. He wasn't totally convinced about that one. He would have a lot of time on his hands.

Jacob was scared but still happy.

The following day Jacob discovered it was hard to do nothing. He thought it best to take a day to collect his thoughts. He tried to sleep later but was only able to stay in bed about an hour more than usual. Showering, shaving and eating breakfast only took another half hour.

Jacob sat back down on the couch and thought: "What's the worse that could happen?" By now even that question failed to hold his attention for very long. He kept coming up with the same consequences from the day before. Eventually his mind would begin to plan out his next actions, an activity he was trying to avoid the first day.

Jacob thought about his encounter with the baker. Yesterday was the first time he'd ever noticed the baker. Jacob went to the kitchen and opened a drawer near the phone. It was crammed with menus from the various restaurants in town.

He quickly paged through them looking for something about the bakery. He was initially unsuccessful so Jacob went through the stack again – this time more deliberate and methodic. Still he found nothing from the baker.

Jacob repacked and closed the drawer. He took the phone book from the top of the refrigerator. The book was faded and covered in a thin film of dust. Jacob wiped the book down with a paper towel and set it on the kitchen table. He flipped the book open to the B's and began searching every ad and listing. He still found no mention of the baker he'd met yesterday.

Jacob was sure the baker's shop had been on Pavilion Avenue. He picked up the phone and dialed the number for information. He gave the operator the name of the town and asked for the number of the bakery on Pavilion Avenue. The operator informed him there was no listing for a bakery on that street or anywhere in the town. She politely suggested several other locations in the surrounding area. Jacob thanked her and hung up.

Shortly after lunch Jacob gave up trying to spend the day on his thoughts and began to make plans for his new life. He had only one rule: be significant. No doubt the manager at his previous job had already shifted his responsibilities to someone else. The quality or productivity might be slightly diminished but he hardly thought anyone would notice. Eventually he'd be replaced permanently or the position simply eliminated.

Still Jacob knew he'd have to find a source of income. There were actually several possibilities, both imaginative and practical. At first he indulged his more fanciful ideas. He could make something and sell it on the Internet. He could invest in some promising new business. He could try painting again.

This inspired Jacob to retrieve some of his artwork from the basement. He stared at the paintings for a long time and wondered if anyone would buy the paintings. How would he sell them? There were no galleries in town. Perhaps he could sell them online. How would anyone find him? As Jacob continued to stare at the paintings he had to admit they were rather childlike and derivative.

He put the paintings aside and turned to more practical thoughts. There were several stores in the area, most of which were always hiring. This was nearly a sure bet but the income would be low and he might not be significant. Still, he was sure his work would have more of a purpose than his previous job.

2.

Jacob left the house without a destination. He took a road leading to the center of town. He wasn't sure why until he turned right on Pavilion Avenue. Jacob walked slowly down the avenue staring at each storefront. He reached the end of the business district without seeing the bakery.

Jacob began to wonder whether or not he was wrong about the street. He had been running from the train station yesterday. Or maybe he had made the whole encounter up in his head.

"Didn't expect to see you so soon," said a familiar voice. Jacob turned around. There was the baker, sweeping in front of the store. "Can you give me a hand?"

Jacob walked back to the baker. He wondered how he could have missed the bakery this time. "I don't think I've ever noticed this shop before," said Jacob.

"Not many do anymore," said the baker. "People buy most of their pies, cakes and cookies from the supermarket on the highway now. They want bread pre-wrapped in plastic that lasts a month. Over time they just forget places like this can exist."

"I saw it yesterday and I was running," replied Jacob.

"Some things you see when you're walking," said the baker. "Other things you only see when you're running." Before Jacob had a chance to reply the baker handed him the broom. "Sweep a little for me?"

Jacob took the broom and started sweeping without giving it much thought. "Broad strokes," said the baker. "A clear path is a sign of a clean shop." The baker went back inside as Jacob continued to sweep.

Jacob looked up at the shop. The windows had become milky with age but he could still make out the counters and shelves inside. The store was long and narrow, set up around a large display case at the back. Shelves flanked the store on both sides. A tall table and three chairs stood in one corner. At the very center of the store, behind the display case was a set of double doors. Jacob supposed the doors led to the kitchen.

"Eyes on your work," said the baker poking his head out of the shop's front door. "Concentrate on what you're doing. Each task is important." He ducked back into the store.

Jacob stared after him for a moment then continued to sweep the front walk and entrance way. As he swept his mind became less cluttered. Thoughts swirling around since he left the house were stirred up and cast off.

"Very good," said the baker. "Come on inside."

Jacob stepped through the front door and immediately felt comfortable and at home. Most of the shelves and the front display case were empty but he could smell the faint aroma of dough in the background. The floor was tiled in one foot square black and white checkers. The side shelves were polished oak carved with ivy branches. The display case seemed to be all glass, a three-dimensional window into a world of sweets and treats.

"Start with the shelves," said the baker. "They need to be cleaned first, then we'll apply a new coat of stain."

"There aren't any items on the shelves." Jacob had skipped breakfast and the dough smell made him feel hungry.

"No" replied the baker. "No baking today – just cleaning. You'll find supplies in the closet." The baker gestured toward a skinny door to the right and back of the store.

Jacob went to the closet. Inside he found a number of different cleaning products, most of which looked like they had been there for several years. "Just use regular soap and water," called the baker from behind him. "That's all you need."

Jacob grabbed a simple bar of soap from the top shelf and placed it in a bucket on the floor of the closet. One side of the closet featured a small but deep sink. The bucket fit perfectly and Jacob filled it with water. As the bucket filled he examined the shelves until he located a hand brush. He grabbed the brush and placed it in the bucket.

Jacob turned the water off and lifted the bucket. It was heavier than he expected and he immediately placed it back on the floor, splashing out some of the water. "Careful," came the baker's voice behind him.

"Maybe I'll just do the floor first," Jacob chuckled.

"We do the floors last," replied the baker sternly.

"Why?" asked Jacob.

"When you clean the shelves you'll push dirt onto the floor. If we did the floors first they would just get dirty again."

"I guess that makes sense," said Jacob.

"Always look for the logical order of things," said the baker. "Now get started on the shelves."

The baker disappeared into the kitchen and Jacob continued to clean the shelves. It took a long time to do it properly but Jacob was happy with the result. He went to the front of the store and tried to look outside one of the windows. It was too cloudy to see out so he pushed the door open. Looking up he could see the sun was now halfway across the horizon.

"Ready to start staining?" asked the baker from behind him.

"Yes," said Jacob closing the door and turning back to the baker. He no longer felt hungry.

"Good," said the baker. "Get a glass of water from the sink first and bring out the stain and rags."

Jacob went back to the closet. An old glass was sitting on the left corner of the sink. He rinsed the glass several times before taking three long drinks from it. He put the glass back down and looked the shelves over once again. Three un-opened cans of stain sat in a neat row on the far right side. A stack of folded rags was to the left of the cans. Jacob picked up the first can of stain and several rags.

"Better get the drop cloths too," suggested the baker. "Stain's hard to get off the floor."

Jacob retrieved the drop cloths from the closet and brought everything over to the nearest of the shelves. He opened the first can and gingerly dipped the rag into it.

"Stay with the grain and try to keep the stain even," advised the baker. "This wood has been stained many times, so it shouldn't soak up too much."

The baker was correct. The stain went on easy and the wood almost immediately looked better. He enjoyed staining much more than cleaning and finished more quickly. When he was done with all the shelves on the right side he took a step back to admire his work.

"Very good," said the baker.

"I was thinking I could just do the floor on this side," said Jacob. "I'd like to see how it all looks finished."

"No," replied the baker. "Do the rest of the staining. "Always batch similar tasks."

"Right," agreed Jacob. He stained the shelves on the other side of the store. By the time he was finished the light outside the store had begun to dim.

"That's enough for today," said the baker. "Go home, eat and get some rest. We'll do the floors and the display case tomorrow."

"Are we going to bake?" asked Jacob.

"First we clean, then we bake," replied the baker.

3.

Jacob was tired and slept later than usual the following morning. Cleaning the store seemed like the hardest day he'd had in a long time. He looked at the clock on his nightstand and saw it was already ten o'clock. He wondered if the baker would be angry. He seemed to remember something about bakers starting very early in the morning.

Jacob dressed hurriedly and quickly walked to Pavilion Street. This time he wasn't careful about looking at each shop for the bakery. He reached the end of the block without finding it. Jacob turned back and went up the street more slowly but he still couldn't find the bakery.

Jacob wandered aimlessly up and down the block until a policeman began eyeing him from across the street. He turned and walked back towards his house. The policeman followed for a few blocks before some high school students attracted his attention. Back at his house Jacob sat down on the faded park bench he kept on the porch.

The postman arrived while he was sitting there. "Morning," said the postman.

"Good morning," returned Jacob. The postman handed him the mail. "Thanks," said Jacob.

"Your welcome," said the postman. "Have a good day."

The postman started to walk away. Jacob jumped up and called after him. "Excuse me," he said.

"Yes?" said the postman turning to face Jacob.

"Do you know the name of the bakery down town?" asked Jacob.

The postman looked up and rested his chin on his hand. He pondered the question for a moment before putting his hand down with a puzzled look on his face. "I didn't know there was a bakery down town," he said.

"It's on Pavilion," said Jacob.

"I don't remember a bakery on Pavilion," said the postman. "But that's not really my route. Did you try calling information?"

"Yes," said Jacob. "They didn't have a number listed. Neither did the phone book."

"Sorry," said the postman. He seemed eager to get on his way. "Lot of deliveries today," he called back over his shoulder as he moved on to the next house.

Jacob settled back down on the bench and glanced at the mail. The first couple of envelopes were clearly solicitations. He threw them aside. Next in the stack was an official looking envelope bearing the return address of his company. Jacob opened up the letter. As he expected, a form letter announced he would be terminated if he did not contact his manager within the next forty-eight hours.

Jacob ripped the letter in half and placed it with the other junk mail. He looked through the rest of the mail, which consisted of two bills and a catalog. He set the catalog aside – he wouldn't be ordering anything for a while. The bills raised the question once again: "What's the worst that could happen?"

He wouldn't be able to pay these bills. They would turn off the electric and the water. However, Jacob knew people who were three months behind on electric and water bills. They hadn't even received collection notices. He wouldn't be able to pay the mortgage when it arrived. Actually, he had just paid the mortgage so it would be almost a month before another bill was even due.

Jacob stuffed the two bills in his pocket and placed the rest of the mail in the garbage can. He left the house and started to walk towards the highway to get something to eat.

Jacob got as far as the bookstore and decided to stop. Once inside he spent a few moments looking over the new releases and flipped through the pages of a new book on art.

It was a book of still life, primarily fruit and other foods. The perspective on each painting was extremely close up. The paintings featured just the outside curve of an apple or the point were two grapes met. They were the kind of paintings Jacob wished he could create. The artwork took a subject captured thousands of times and presented it in a totally new light.

Jacob carried the book with him as he moved deeper into the store's interior. He continued to flip through the pages as he walked. "Watch out," called out a young woman's voice.

Jacob looked up just as he walked into a display near the front of an isle. Several of the books toppled over and he heard a large sigh from one of the bookstore employees. "Are you okay?" asked the same young woman.

"Yes. Thanks," replied Jacob. "I guess I wasn't watching where I was going." He started to pick up the books and place them back on the display.

"I guess not," replied the woman. "A good book can have that effect on you."

"Yes," replied Jacob. He tried to think of a clever return. Jacob gestured to the book and said, "I like art."

"Good for you," said the young woman. She giggled as she walked away.

He shook his head and put the last book back on the display. As he set it down he saw it was a book on soups. Jacob looked at the isle in front of him and discovered he had wandered into the cooking section. Near the center of the isle was an area of books on baking.

Jacob spent the next hour looking through books on breads, pies, cookies and cakes. He read about the chemistry of bread rising. He learned the difference between a morning and an evening pastry. He found the definition for marzipan. He saw the many ways that flour, butter and eggs could be combined and reconstituted. Jacob saw art.

4.

When Jacob woke up promptly at six the next morning his head was still full of cookies, cobbler and croissant. The clock on the wall reminded him of a bagel; he imagined his toothpaste was an éclair. It was well before seven when he arrived on Pavilion Avenue, out of breath from running all the way from the house.

"Seven will do for now," said the baker. "Five or six would be better. Always start early and work on the hardest parts first."

Jacob nodded, out of breath. He was just glad to see the baker again.

"Come inside and we'll start on the display case," said the baker. Jacob followed him into the bakery.

"This display case is very old," explained the baker. "The center display is where you'll place your signature creations - those items of which you are most proud."

Jacob walked over to the case with glass cleaner and several fresh rags. The baker held up his hand.

"No rags for this job," he said. "On the top shelf of the closet you'll find a small velvet sack. Within the sack is a special cloth. The cloth is woven to be extremely smooth."

"So we don't scratch the glass," replied Jacob.

"Exactly," said the baker. "Use that and the cleaner. Spray the cleaner onto the glass and gently rub with the cloth. Rub in circles and be sure to remove all the liquid."

Jacob retrieved the cloth and cleaned the case as the baker instructed him. Through the glass the case was empty but inviting. "What do you keep in the case?" he asked the baker.

"My best work," replied the baker. He lightly rubbed his hand across the display case.

Jacob looked into the case as he cleaned and tried to imagine the baker's wares. For a moment he thought cakes but for some reason that didn't seem right. Then he saw all kinds of pies. Each had its own special design on top. Some were crisscrossed by strips of dough. Others were solid with just a few slits at regular intervals. There were meringues and custards with whipped tops and open pies with mounds of chopped fruit.

"That's much better," said the baker. Jacob had reached the opposite end of case. He stood back up and looked at his work. The display case was almost like new. "Now we can do the floors," announced the baker.

Jacob returned the cloth to its velvet bag and placed it back on the top shelf of the closet. He put the glass cleaner back as well and grabbed the bucket. It still had the bar of soap at the bottom so he merely had to fill it with water. While it was filling he grabbed the mop from the corner.

The floor was not very dirty so Jacob was able to make fast work of it. Once finished he looked up at the baker behind the display case who nodded approvingly. "Should I do the windows and the door next?" asked Jacob.

"Not yet," said the baker.

"But the windows are murky," protested Jacob. "No one can see inside."

"Do we have anything to show them yet?" asked the baker. "Is there anything on our shelves or in our case?"

"No," replied Jacob.

"Then there is no need to clean the windows...yet," said the baker. "Bring the bucket and mop and we'll start on the kitchen."

The kitchen looked extremely clean and orderly. Still, the baker told Jacob to go over everything with the soap and water for good measure. "It is an opportunity for you to learn the kitchen," said the baker. "Pay attention to the location of everything. Learn the controls of the oven and stove. Look for the slope and angle of each counter top. Feel the grain of the wood in the chopping block."

Jacob cleaned the entire kitchen with soap and water, taking care to remember as much about everything as possible. The equipment was older but sturdy. It had character and he liked it very much. Jacob cleaned each of the spoons, spatulas and other utensils hanging around the kitchen.

"Each of those has a purpose," said the baker as Jacob cleaned off a small spoon. "Just like the special cloth for the display case. Always use the right tool for the right job."

Jacob nodded and continued to work his way through the various implements. He wanted to ask the baker about each one. He knew that would slow the work down, though.

"You will learn about each of those as we use it," said the baker as if sensing Jacob's curiosity.

It took several hours to wipe down and rinse the kitchen. The light outside was once again fading. Jacob thought about the previous day. What if he arrived tomorrow and couldn't find the bakery again?

"Don't worry," said the baker. "As long as you do the right things, the bakery will always be here for you."

"Will we bake tomorrow?" asked Jacob.

"Soon," replied the baker. "Now that we have cleaned, we are almost ready."

"I didn't see any ingredients," said Jacob.

"Go to the center of the cutting table," replied the baker. "Open the drawer there. Inside you will find a list of supplies and addresses. Go to each address and you will find the items listed below it."

Jacob looked through the list. It was several hand-written pages. Each page began with an address. Following the address was a list of ingredients. Under the first address were a variety of flours, powders and grains. The next address listed spices. Fruits and vegetables were on the following page. The last page listed several dairy items. At the very bottom of each page was the same signature. It was highly stylized so Jacob could not make out the name.

"Show each merchant the signature on the bottom of the pages," said the baker. "They will help you." The baker walked him out through the kitchen doors and into the front of the store. "Get an early start and bring everything to the shop when you are finished. I won't expect you until the afternoon."

5.

Jacob fell asleep that night reading through the books he'd purchased. In his dreams he saw the baker in his shop. The baker was carefully trimming the excess crust off the edges of a pie. He took the remaining bits of dough and balled them in his hands. The baker rolled the dough back out and used a knife to carve out several shapes. He used the shapes to create a design that looked like ivy on top of the pie.

"Watch out for the fox," the baker said as he placed the pie in the oven. Those words stayed with Jacob as the rest of the dream faded. Leaving his house that day he was excited and nervous at the same time. He looked at the list again as he walked to his car. He decided to follow the order of the pages exactly as they were written.

Several other people were already at the flour vender when Jacob arrived. Many were dressed as chefs. Others were dressed in blue work suits bearing the logo of the vender. Almost everyone was yelling out a request or a response.

"I need ten pounds of the wheat!" yelled one chef.

"Do you have any more of that mixed grain from last week?" shouted another.

Jacob looked down at the first item on his list. He started to open his mouth but shut it quickly and stared back down at the list. The baker didn't describe anything like this. Jacob had envisioned walking up to a counter and passing the list across it. Now he was at what looked like a loading dock, surrounded by tens of people who all knew much more than him. More than once he got a disapproving look from a worker or one of the chefs.

"Get out of my way," said one of the chefs shoving him aside. "I need to make an 11am sitting."

The shove caused him to crash into a worker pushing a hand truck with several bags of baking flour. "What are you doing?" the worker barked at him.

"I'm sorry," Jacob mumbled. In the crash he had lost the baker's list. He dropped to his knees and frantically searched for it. "My list..."

"Is this yours, son?" a voice asked from above him.

Jacob stood up to face an older man in the same blue uniform as the other workers. The man still had a strong build but hair long gone gray. He wore a pair of reading glasses three-quarters of the way down his nose. He held Jacob's now semi-rumpled list in his hand and stared at him over top of the glasses.

"Yes," said Jacob. "Thank you."

"First time here?" asked the man.

"Yes. I'm not really sure..." began Jacob.

"Name's Harley," said the man shaking Jacob's hand. "I'm old enough to remember the first day of most of these other chefs."

"Thanks," said Jacob handing over his list.

"Let's just see what we've got here," said Harley. The old man lowered his eyes so he could look through the spectacles at the list. He read over the first page, lingering over the signature at the bottom. He looked up over the glasses again and eyed up Jacob.

"Wait here," said Harley. He walked away with the baker's list.

Jacob stared after him until he could no longer see the man in the crowd. Then he flopped down on a nearby crate. What's the worst that could happen? He would be accused of stealing the baker's list. He would be arrested, possibly even suspected of murdering the baker. He would go to jail. At least then he wouldn't have to worry about paying the bills.

"You should be all set," said Harley.

Jacob looked up to see the man had returned with three other men. Each had a hand truck filled with sacks of flour, baking powder and other ingredients. "Where's your vehicle?" asked Harley.

"Over there," Jacob stammered. "What do I owe..."

"Everything's done on account," explained the man. "We settle up with the bakery at the end of the month." He handed Jacob back the list. "See you next month," he said as the men loaded the supplies in Jacob's car.

To Jacob's relief the spice vender was a much more relaxed environment. This time he did find himself in a more traditional shop. It wasn't large but the walls were covered in shelves holding every type of spice, herb and seasoning imaginable. The three small center isles had over-sized and odd shaped items such as whole branches of bushes.

At the back of the store a short, stout man sat on a stool behind a waste high counter. He wore a tag inscribed with the name "Tovold." A sign hung above his head proclaimed: "WHOLESALE AVAILABLE. BAKERS AND CHEFS WELCOME."

Jacob confidently strode to the back of the store and up to the counter. "Hello," said Tovold. "What can I do for you?"

Jacob looked down at the second page on his list and started to read off the names and quantities. He only recognized a couple of the spices such as cinnamon and cumin but he tried to read confidently.

"Hold on," interrupted Tovold. "Those are wholesale quantities. You don't look like a baker to me."

"I'm not," said Jacob. "At least not yet."

"Are you selling these online?" asked Tovold.

"No," replied Jacob. This had suddenly gotten harder than the flour distributor. "I have this list," he said, placing the list on the counter.

The man behind the counter snatched the list from him and began looking it over. Several times he looked back up at Jacob. "I don't know," mumbled the man. "These are large quantities. You don't look like a baker."

When Tovold got to the signature at the bottom of the list he paused. He lifted the list and held it up in front of the light. For the first time Jacob saw there was a watermark underneath the whole paper. It was three strands of crossed ivy. The stout man put the list back on the counter and looked at the signature again. He traced its curves with his finger.

"I know this signature," said Tovold. "You're not a baker yet...but you will be. Wait here." The man took the list and disappeared into a back room. He returned a couple of minutes later with two boxes, one of which was filled to the top. The man took the other box and began walking up and down the isles of the store. Jacob watched as he took an item from here or there and added it to the box.

When the second box was full he returned to the counter. Tovold pushed the boxes forward to Jacob. "Learn the tastes of every item in the boxes," he said. "Then learn how each one tastes together."

Jacob nodded and picked up the boxes. "Settle up at the end of the month?" he asked tentatively.

"Of course," said Tovold. As Jacob started to walk out the stout man called after him. "And next time come here first. You'll avoid the rush at the flour distributor."

Jacob's next stop was the fruit distributor. He thought about the spice vender's suggestion to go there first and wondered about the other stops. He remembered something in one of the books about getting to the fruit and vegetable stand as early as possible to get first choice. If the people at this vender seemed friendly enough Jacob decided he would ask about it.

The scene at the fruit distributor contained as many people as the flour vender but it was much more organized. Chefs and other customers wound their way in and around the isles in an orderly fashion. Across from them several workers wrote down orders. Customers would pick up a fruit or two from each bunch and examine them. They would say something like "if all the peppers are this firm I'll take three bushels" or "next time not so ripe" or "this will be spoiled by the dinner service."

Jacob got into the winding line and started to examine the fruit. He had no idea what he was doing but tried to follow the actions and assessments of the customers ahead of him. He requested some apples but rejected some pears, unsure of why he did either. A couple of times he noticed the woman to his left smiling.

"First time?" asked the woman.

Jacob looked at her. She seemed non-threatening enough so he answered "yes."

"Thought so," replied the woman. "Did the sous chef send you?"

"No," said Jacob. "I work for a baker."

"I see," said the woman. "Paul?" she called out to one of the men taking orders. "Why don't you help this young gentlemen so he doesn't make a fool of himself. I don't know what kind of a baker would send a novice out to pick fruit."

"Come over here and let me see your list," said the man apparently called Paul. Jacob met Paul at the end of the isle and gave him the list. The man stared at the list for a few moments and held the pages up to the light as the spice vender had done. When he saw the ivy watermark he told Jacob to wait a minute and walked inside with the list.

A moment later a middle-aged woman came outside and walked over to Jacob with the list. She held it up to the light. "I've never seen this seal, but my father told me about it. Bring your truck over to the side and we'll take care of your list."

"Don't I need to pick out..." said Jacob.

The woman looked over at the line of people looking through the fruit. "You mean all that poking and prodding?" She laughed. "If you pick the right supplier from the start you always know the fruit is good. And we always reserve our best fruit for our best customers."

Jacob thought about the baker as he drove to the dairy distributor. Everyone seemed to know his signature and seal. He wondered about the significance of the ivy carved into the wooden shelves and embedded into the watermark of the paper...and ivy designs on the tops of pies. He now recalled that part of his dream.

The dairy distributor came up sooner than he expected and he missed the entrance. Jacob did a quick turn into the next driveway so he could turn around. Once in the driveway a man in a denim shirt approached him.

"Good day," said the man in the denim shirt.

"Hello," said Jacob.

"Looking for milk and eggs?" the man asked.

"Yes," replied Jacob. "I just missed the turn for the dairy."

"This is the dairy," said the man. He pointed to a sign at the right of the drive. Jacob looked at the sign and glanced at the list on the seat next to him. The name and address did not match.

"I'm sorry," said Jacob. "I'm supposed to go to the other dairy."

"You don't want to go there," said the man. "He charges double for the same milk. Half of his eggs are cracked. Pull up and we'll take care of you."

Jacob was unsure what to do. He was sure the baker knew best but was embarrassed about turning around in the other dairy's drive. How different was the milk from one dairy to another? Wouldn't the baker appreciate him saving some money?

Jacob remembered what the woman at the fruit distributor said: her father had told her about the signature. That meant the baker hadn't been out to pick up supplies himself in a long time. Perhaps he didn't know about the other, cheaper dairy.

"Ok," said Jacob. He drove up to the main building at the end of the driveway. The man followed him on foot. When they reached the top of the drive he yelled something in another language and several men ran over. The man gave them a series of instructions and they went into the building.

The man lit a cigarette while they were waiting. "First time picking up the supplies?" he asked.

"Yes," said Jacob.

"So are you like an apprentice or just a stock boy?" asked the man in the denim shirt between puffs.

Jacob thought about this for a moment. So far he had cleaned the entire bakery and ran around picking up supplies. That didn't sound like much of an apprentice.

"Stock boy, huh?" The man smiled and took a long drag from the cigarette. He yelled something else in the other language. A moment later the men came out of the building carrying racks of milk and several cartons of eggs. Jacob looked at the list and started counting.

"I'm giving you the cash discount," said the man.

Jacob looked up from his counting. "Cash?" he asked. One of the men started loading a tray of milk into the front seat of his car. The backseat was already filled with fruit and spices.

"That's right," said the man in the denim shirt. Can't do end of the month for a new customer. Besides, I can offer you a better price for cash now."

Jacob looked at the man's eyes. The man turned his head and blew out a cloud of smoke. Without turning back he said, "Didn't want to blow smoke at you."

Jacob looked down at the tray of milk about to be loaded into his car. The date on the milk bottles indicated they would expire the next day. "I'm sorry," said Jacob. "I don't have cash. I'll have to go to the other dairy."

Without another word Jacob got back into the car. He backed up and quickly made his way back down the drive. The man glared at him, then shouted something else at the men. They all scattered.

Jacob continued on his way back to the other dairy. He thought about the ivy pattern on the tops of the pies and about he baker's words: "Watch out for the fox."

6.

Jacob was exhausted by the time he got home. He was even too tired to look through his books on baking. After picking up all the supplies he drove them back to the bakery and carried them inside. Once in the kitchen the baker had a place and position for everything. He instructed Jacob to unload slowly and concentrate on where everything was kept.

Flour went in the bottom section of the main pantry. Ripe fruits were stacked in the cool pantry according to type. Unripe fruits were placed in several hanging baskets throughout the kitchen. Spices and herbs were placed in their own series of cabinets, sorted by flavor type.

"Always make sure you are ready for ingredients to mix," said the baker.

Jacob thought about the foods he'd delivered to the bakery while rummaging around his own kitchen for something to eat. It appeared he had nothing in the house. Most days he simply picked something up on the way home from work. It was rare for him to cook anything. That would all change tomorrow.

But tonight Jacob would have to go back out and buy something for dinner. He reluctantly went back to his car. It still smelled like fruit and spices. The smell was pleasant although a bit overwhelming and Jacob imagined how those smells might come together in cake or pie.

As he drove, Jacob scanned the various restaurant signs looking for something he was hungry for at the moment. Not far up the road he came across a car dealership. This reminded him of his earlier idea of trading in the new car for something less expensive. He was sure he was too tired to worry about it this evening until he saw the truck.

The white pickup looked about ten years old. The recently washed paint and higher profile stood out among the smaller vehicles around it. Jacob turned the car into the parking lot and stopped near the main building.

Jacob walked back to the truck and looked at the price. Although the truck had held value the price was well below what he'd paid for his car. Swapping it out would cut his monthly payment by half. It would also be more practical for the bakery.

"Excellent condition, isn't it?" said a voice behind him.

Jacob turned around to face the salesman, who'd come up behind him. Jacob knew better than to betray too much emotion. "Looks okay," he said. "How many miles?"

"Seventy-five thousand," said the salesman. "These models go around two hundred, though. Looking for a second vehicle?"

"Trade in," said Jacob.

"Trading for that?" asked the salesman gesturing back at Jacob's car. Jacob could see the excitement in the salesman's eyes at the prospect. His car was a popular model that was selling well – even used.

"Yes. The car's not practical for my new job," said Jacob.

"What do you do?" asked the salesman.

"I'm a baker's apprentice," replied Jacob.

"Why don't we take a drive in it," suggested the salesman.

The salesman retrieved the keys to the truck and took Jacob for a test drive. As they drove the salesman continued to explain the features and benefits of the vehicle. Everything just seemed to fit. Despite his efforts to contain it, Jacob was smiling by the time they got back to the lot.

"Come on inside," said the salesman. "Let's see what we can work out."

Jacob continued to drive the truck for another couple of hours after leaving the lot. He decided he wasn't sorry to have gotten rid of the car. He'd bought it on the spur of the moment after a bad day at work. It was just one more attempt to add meaning to his old life. The only thing he missed about the car was the aroma from the day's errands.

On the way home Jacob drove down Pavilion Avenue. He couldn't make out the bakery from the street. He tried to remember if he'd ever stopped to look at the bakery at the end of the day. The shop was most noticeable in the early morning, especially when he was excited and running towards it.

Jacob decided it was probably the murky windows that made the bakery hard to see from the street. A few of the other storefronts on the same street were also vacant. He supposed they all started to blend together, especially if you were in motion. The bakery would be noticeable after they cleaned the windows.

The baker's words came back to him. "Do we have anything to show them yet?" asked the baker. "Is there anything on our shelves or in our case?"

"No," said Jacob out loud. "Until we have something to show there is no reason to clean the windows."

In his mind the baker seemed to agree. "What is a bakery without cakes and pies and cookies?" he would say.

7.

"Good dough is the foundation for everything we create," explained the baker. "If the dough isn't right, nothing will work. You must learn to make good dough first."

"How long will it take me to learn to make the dough?" asked Jacob.

"It will take as long as it takes," replied the baker. "Always take the time to learn a skill right."

"Go to the pantry and get the flour, salt and yeast," instructed the baker. Jacob retrieved the items as instructed and placed them on the counter.

"What else do I need?" he Jacob.

"That is all for now," said the baker.

"We're going to make dough from just these three things?" asked Jacob.

"Oh yes," said the baker, "we'll need some warm water."

Jacob went to the facet and ran the water for a few moments until it began to get hotter. "How warm?" he asked.

"Luke warm is fine," said the baker. "Feel your arm."

Jacob felt his arm and turned to the baker. "When it feels as warm as your arm," said the baker, "it's ready."

Jacob brought the water over to other ingredients on the counter. He looked at the baker for further instruction.

"Mix the yeast with the water," instructed the baker. Jacob mixed the yeast with the water until it dissolved. "Good," said the baker. "Now take some of the flour and make a small mound out of it."

Jacob began to clumsily pile up the flour. The baker shook his head. "You're not concentrating enough," he said.

"It's just a mound," said Jacob. He tried to pile up the flour in random sweeping motions.

"Making dough is deceptively simple," explained the baker. "There are only four ingredients and six steps. But the simplicity makes each of the elements that much more important."

"How can it be simple and complex?" asked Jacob. In his mind he had pictured large mixing bowls, big metal spoons and a vast array of exotic ingredients. He looked down at the lop-sided mound of flour.

"Flour, water, yeast and salt," continued the baker. "The importance of a thing is more than just its complexity and the complexity of a thing is more than just the number of its parts."

Jacob thought about this for a moment. He had always been taught the importance of a job was related to the number of your responsibilities. The more you had to do the more important you must be.

"Who is more important," asked the baker, "the man who does many of the least important jobs or the man who does the few most important jobs?"

"I suppose the second man," said Jacob.

"Making the dough is the most important job," said the baker. "Flour, water, yeast and salt are the most important ingredients."

"I see," said Jacob.

"There are only six steps," continued the baker. "Mix, mound, knead, rise, punch and rise again. But that makes each step very important. Mounding is just as important as rising or kneading."

"I think I understand," said Jacob. He began to shape the flour into a mound again, this time much more deliberately and carefully.

"Good," said the baker. "Do not be distracted; do not rush. Always concentrate on the task at hand as if it is the most important."

"Because in that moment it is the most important," added Jacob.

"That is right," said the baker with a smile. "You are ready for the next step. Make a small pocket in the center of your mound."

Jacob followed the baker's instructions. "Pour in the water?" he asked.

"Yes," replied the baker. Jacob poured the water into the center of mound. "Now place some flour on your hands and begin to knead the dough. Push the dough away with the heels of your hands. Then pick up the opposite edge and fold it toward you."

Jacob tried pushing and folding the dough a couple of times with limited success. "You're rushing again," corrected the baker. "Go slower and concentrate on each move. Push and fold. Push and fold."

Jacob did as the baker instructed and started to maintain a steady rhythm in his kneading. "How long?" he asked.

"What does it matter?" asked the baker.

"But how do I know when it's ready?" asked Jacob.

"When it feels ready," said the baker. "It should be soft and smooth but not too dry. It stops sticking to your hands and springs back to the touch."

"Okay," said Jacob. "If it gets too dry should I add more water?"

"Kneading is about balance," explained the baker. "The right amount of flour, the right amount of water and the right amount of air."

"Air?" asked Jacob.

"Yes," answered the baker. "While you knead you allow air into the dough. The air is food for the yeast and provides a better rise."

The dough felt dry so Jacob added more water. This made it feel too wet so he added more flour.

"Are you feeling with your heart, your head or your hands?" asked the baker.

"My head," said Jacob. "No wait, probably my heart."

"When kneading, feel with your hands," said the baker.

"Oh," said Jacob.

"You'll know when to use your heart and head," said the baker. "For now add a pinch more flour and you should be back in balance."

After around ten minutes the dough started to feel right to Jacob. "I think it's ready," he said and looked at the baker tentatively.

"Good," said the baker. "Shape it into a ball and place it in that bowl. Cover the bowl and allow the dough to rise."

"How long?" asked Jacob. He regretted asking as soon as the words were out of his mouth.

The baker laughed. "Until the dough doubles in size," said the baker. "Probably about two hours."

"I suppose we need to be patient," said Jacob.

"Yes," said the baker. "Or we could make up a batch of sweet dough while we wait."

8.

Jacob stared at the batches of dough lined up on the counter against the wall. He had made five additional ones while the first batch was rising. The techniques were the same, only the ingredients slightly different.

"Think about how the various ingredients change the feel of the dough," said the baker. "You must learn how to read the various types. Different consistencies give you different results."

"Is that why bread tastes so different place to place?" asked Jacob.

"And looks and feels different," added the baker.

Jacob took the towel off the first bowl and looked at the dough. It had risen to about twice its original size. "I think it's ready to bake," declared Jacob.

"Not yet," said the baker. "That's just the first rise. Remember the six steps. Punch is next. Punch the dough back down and allow it rise again."

Jacob removed the dough from the bowl and punched it repeatedly until it had shrunk once again. "That's good," said the baker. "Split the batch into several balls and place them in separate bowls to rise again."

Jacob formed the dough into four balls and looked at the baker for approval. The baker nodded and Jacob continued to place the dough into bowls. "Do you think the next batch is ready?" asked Jacob.

"Check and see," said the baker.

Jacob glanced under the covered bowl holding the sweet dough. "Not quite yet," he said.

"Give it a few more minutes," said the baker. "Eventually you'll be able to time everything out."

"Always batch your tasks," said Jacob.

"Exactly," agreed the baker.

A few minutes later Jacob was able to punch down the sweet dough. "Try shaping it into a twist," suggested the baker. Jacob stretched the dough out and twisted it into a rudimentary shape before placing it back for its second rise. While they waited for the dough to rise the second time the baker talked Jacob through cutting up several pieces of fruit. He also had Jacob taste several pieces.

"Fillings taste different depending on how ripe the fruit is when you cook it," explained the baker. "Did you notice how the taste of the previous fruit lingered when you tasted the next one?"

"Yes," said Jacob.

"You can combine flavors the same way in your fillings," said the baker. "Taste your combinations uncooked first. Then taste again after cooking. "

"How do I make the raw fruit into a filling?" asked Jacob.

"We'll do that another day," said the baker. "Today you should concentrate on your dough. Master the dough then move on to the fillings and toppings. Besides, I believe the dough is almost finished its second rise."

"What about all the fruit?" asked Jacob.

"Place the pieces in covered bowls and put them in the refrigerator for later. Feel free to mix some of your favorite combinations. Once you're finished you should be ready to bake.

"Heat is another way you can influence the dough," said the baker as Jacob placed some of the original dough into a pan for baking. "Every oven cooks differently."

"You mean some ovens are hotter than others?" asked Jacob.

"Not quite," said the baker. "Each oven contains areas that are hotter than others."

"Can't they make an oven that cooks more evenly?" asked Jacob.

"I suppose they could," said the baker. "But it would remove some of the artistry of baking. We can use hot and cold areas of the oven to our advantage."

"How?" asked Jacob.

"We can control the rate at which the dough bakes by moving it around the oven at different times," explained the baker. "If we want a crispy crust with a chewy inside we can start the dough at a less hot area of the oven where it cooks slower. Then we could move the dough to another area of the oven that will cook the outside faster."

"I see," said Jacob. He pointed at the oven. "Where are the hotter areas in this oven?"

"I could tell you," answered the baker, "but it would be better for you to learn them on your own. Tomorrow you will bake several loafs of bread in different parts of the oven for the same amount of time."

"I'll be able to tell the hotter areas by the way the bread cooks," said Jacob.

"Yes," said the baker. "Now let's bake your first loaf of bread."

Sometime later Jacob was able to take a bite. "It's really not that good," he said.

"Describe the taste," said the baker.

"Bland yet salty," said Jacob.

The baker chuckled. "Good. If you can identify the taste you can correct the problem," he said. "You probably added too much salt."

"I understand that," said Jacob. "Why is it bland, though?"

"It's bland because it did not ferment enough," explained the baker.

"That has to do with the yeast, right?" suggested Jacob.

"Yes," said the baker. "You must knead the dough better to allow more air bubbles. Remember the yeast feeds on the air. If it starves, you starve."

"Okay," said Jacob.

"You also need to punch and shape the dough down better," continued the baker. "You did not allow it to rest enough."

"It has to rest?" asked Jacob.

"Between risings, yes," confirmed the baker. "Yeast is a living thing. You need to treat it as such."

Jacob looked down at the bread feeling very disheartened. "Don't worry," said the baker. "You're off to an excellent start. Many people cannot even get the first loaf to rise. Try your sweat bread."

Jacob tried a bit of the sweet bread and found it a bit better. "Probably because it's sweeter," he said.

"Taste again," said the baker.

Jacob chewed another bit of the sweet bread. "This is definitely better," he confirmed. "Not just because of the eggs and butter."

"Exactly," agreed the baker. "You were better with your second loaf. You'll always have setbacks, but for the most part you'll get better each time you bake. It's been a long productive day. Why don't you clean up for now?"

Jacob washed the used bowls and wiped the counters. "Go home and get some rest," said the baker. "We'll continue tomorrow."

9.

Jacob was tired when he got home but he couldn't seem to rest. He spent some time going through the mail. As usual, most of it was not important. However, there was a letter from his company announcing he had been formally terminated for non-attendance. His departure was now official.

Jacob wandered into his kitchen. A bag of flour and a few packets of yeast were on the counter. Without thinking about it, Jacob took out a handful of flour and spread it loosely on the counter top. He hand scooped several more clumps of flour and formed it into a mound.

Several hours and several batches later his hands were too tired to continue kneading the dough. Exhausted, he walked out of the kitchen and into the bedroom. Jacob instantly fell asleep on his bed. He only slept for a short time before the alarm went off. Still in a daze Jacob left the house and shuffled down town to the bakery.

Jacob hobbled into the kitchen of the bakery and slumped down on a stool. The baker looked him over. "There's more flour on you than in the dough," he said.

Jacob looked down at his hands. They were still covered in flour from the night before. In fact, most of him was covered in flour. His pants and shirt looked slightly bleached and tiny clots of white clung to the hair on his arms. "Did you bake all night?" asked the baker.

"I guess so," said Jacob.

"Then you need to sleep," replied the baker. "Go home and rest up. After a few hours, do some more practicing at home. Go to bed at a decent time tonight and we'll start with the oven tomorrow."

Jacob paused just before leaving the kitchen of the bakery. "Are you mad?" he asked the baker.

"Mad?" replied the baker. "Young man, the one thing I can't teach you is enthusiasm."

Jacob felt much better after a few hours sleep. He made himself something to eat and went back to practicing with the dough. He began to get a much better feel for how long to knead but he was still having trouble with the measurements. Almost every batch he needed to add a bit more water or a bit more flour. Usually he would over compensate and his batches came out much larger than he originally intended.

The mounds of dough he'd created throughout the day and previous night gave him an idea. Tomorrow they were going to test the oven for the hotter areas. That would require several loaves. Jacob decided he would bring in the dough he'd made and they could use that to test the oven.

This gave him another idea. He marked the batches to indicate in what order he'd created them. This would allow him to see if he'd really made any progress. Jacob packaged up the various batches and placed them in the refrigerator before going back to bed.

The next morning he felt much better as he made his way to the bakery. "What's all this?" asked the baker as Jacob entered the kitchen with his arms full of plastic containers.

"I thought I might use my test batches for our oven experiments," replied Jacob.

"Excellent idea," said the baker. "You've already started thinking ahead of me."

Jacob put the batches into pans and the baker instructed him on the proper way to turn on the oven. "It will take awhile to heat up," said the baker.

"Normally you should turn the oven on first thing when you arrive."

Jacob wondered why the baker hadn't turned on the oven when he arrived. He decided not to worry about it. He probably wanted Jacob to practice the controls. "What should we do while we wait?"

"We'll talk a little more about flour," said the baker. "How would you describe bread?"

"Brown on the outside, white on the inside," answered Jacob. "Every loaf is different, I guess."

"That's the physical description," said the baker. "But how would you describe bread as a food?"

Jacob thought for a moment. "It's a staple, I guess. Bread is always there. It accompanies the meal."

"In days past bread was the meal," added the baker. "Bread contains basic elements we need such as protein. Bread gives us life."

"That makes sense," agreed Jacob.

"Now describe cake," said the baker.

"Cake is dessert," said Jacob. "It's the best part of the meal."

"Exactly," said the baker. "We eat bread to live but we live to eat cake."

"I think I understand," said Jacob.

"Cake doesn't have as much protein," continued the baker. "But it tastes better than the bread."

"What does this have to do with flour?" asked Jacob.

"There are two types of flour," explained the baker. "One type contains a lot of protein. We use that flour to create bread and pasta. The other type contains less protein. We use that flour to create cakes and pies."

"I see," said Jacob.

"Always know what you want to create before you start," said the baker.

When it was time, Jacob pulled down the oven door and peeked in at the loaves. "The ones on the middle left side look almost done," he said. "That must be the hottest area of the oven."

"Good," said the baker. "Where is it the least hot?"

"Right front corner," answered Jacob.

"What about the other areas?" asked the baker.

"The front is slightly cooler," said Jacob. "The left side is hotter than the right. The middle is also hotter."

"You're doing fine," said the baker. "As you bake you'll find the temperatures are even more subtle than they appear now. Use this to your advantage."

"How do I know how long to leave something in any one area of the oven?" asked Jacob.

"You'll just have to experiment," said the baker. "Experimenting is the best part of baking. Those are the times when you'll truly create something new."

10.

"Always taste your own work," said the baker.

Jacob took a bite of the cookies he'd just pulled out of the oven. "Needs more cinnamon," he said.

"Try sprinkling some on top," suggested the baker.

Jacob sprinkled additional cinnamon on top of the cookie and took another bite. "Better," he confirmed.

"Did you notice anything else?" asked the baker.

"The texture is a bit different," said Jacob.

"And?" prompted the baker.

"The cinnamon had a bit more bite," answered Jacob.

"Why?" asked the baker.

"Because it was right on my tongue," said Jacob.

'That's correct," confirmed the baker. "A whole is not just the sum of its parts. It is also the order of its parts. Adding the cinnamon at the end has a different effect than adding it to the batter."

Jacob nodded. He looked around the kitchen. It was now filled with all types of breads, pies, cookies and cakes. The smells he'd noticed the first day he'd entered the bakery were now right on the surface. Jacob took a deep breath. He had been working with the baker for over two weeks now. Jacob felt he'd learned more during that time than he had over the last few years.

"You should never stop learning," said the baker. "But there is one more thing you must learn now."

"Yes?" asked Jacob.

"Presentation," said the baker. "Always present your creations honestly but with flair." The baker gestured toward the doors to the front part of the shop.

Jacob picked up the two trays nearest him and carried them out to the front of the building. He initially set the trays down on the top of the glass counter and paused for several minutes.

"What's wrong?" asked the baker.

"You told me a baker places his best creations in the glass counter," said Jacob. "But I don't know what my best is yet. How do I know what to put under the glass?"

"That is something you won't know for awhile," replied the baker. "When you were making dough you used your hands to make decisions. Now you should use your head. Eventually you'll use your heart."

"I guess I'll put the breads on the side isles," said Jacob, "and the cookies and cakes in the display case."

"Logical choice," said the baker. "There are baskets to hold the breads in the kitchen closet."

Jacob went back to the kitchen and located the collection of baskets. They were exactly the right size for the shelves. He arranged the baskets on the shelves and then started moving the bread out to the front of the store. After he finished with the breads he brought the sweets out to the glass display counter.

"It's not the best layout," acknowledged Jacob looking around.

"No," agreed the baker. "But it is functional. Unartistic but orderly is better than disorderly but artistic."

"We want people to find what they're looking for," said Jacob.

"Yes," said the baker. "But you should also help them anticipate what they want or need. Know the store, know your creations and know your customers. Then you will be able to offer help."

Jacob supposed the baker was right in most cases but he was still skeptical. "But not everyone wants to be helped," he still protested.

"That is why I say to know your customers," said the baker. "Learn to read who needs help and who doesn't and remember that needs are different than wants."

"What's the difference?" asked Jacob.

"Many times a customer needs help even if they don't appear to want it," said the baker.

"How can I tell that?" asked Jacob.

"Watch their eyes," said the baker.

"It sounds difficult," replied Jacob.

"Making the dough was difficult as well," answered the baker. "But then you practiced and it got easier."

"True enough," said Jacob.

The baker was silent for a few moments and Jacob leaned back against the glass counter, taking in the sights and smells of the newly filled shop. Finally the baker spoke again. "Is there a shelter or food bank near here?" he asked.

"Not in town," answered Jacob. "But one of the local churches collects food for a shelter in the city."

"Good," replied the baker. "Round up all the cooked food from the shelves and case. Take it over to the church. Always give away that which you have in excess."

"Aren't we going to sell this?" protested Jacob.

"This," said the baker gesturing at the food around the shop "was practice. Where is the last loaf of bread you baked?"

Jacob held up the last loaf he'd baked. "This is it," he said.

"Would you want to sell someone that loaf?" asked the baker.

"Yes," said Jacob. "I'm sure I'll get better but this one is very good." He was insulted by the way the baker was acting. Didn't he see how far he'd come in the last couple of weeks?

"Now hold up the earliest one you baked," said the baker.

Jacob walked over to another part of the shelf and picked up the loaf. He could see immediately it was a bit misshapen and had slightly collapsed on one side. "Here," he said.

"Would you want to sell someone that loaf?" asked the baker.

"Not really," said Jacob.

"Of course not," said the baker. "Always sell only items worthy of your craft."

"Okay," said Jacob. He began to gather up the food in the bakery. "All of it?" he asked the baker.

"Yes," said the baker. "It's better to start fresh. Tomorrow we begin for real. When you're finished with that, you can clean off the windows."

11.

The next morning was an exciting one for Jacob. He arrived at the bakery even earlier than usual. He started the oven immediately and began making the first batch of dough. He grouped his tasks as the baker had taught him, making several balls of bread dough first. After that he made the sweeter bread batches. Jacob cleaned off the counter and started on dough for muffins and pastry.

While the dough was rising he cut up several fruits and mixed them with water and sugar to create the fillings. Jacob went to the oven and checked the temperature. It was now warm.

Jacob initially made two trays of bagels and two trays of muffins. "Breakfast foods move first," explained the baker. "Bagels, muffins and danish are purchased at the start of the day. Cakes and cookies are purchased at the end of the day."

Jacob had just finished laying out the last of the breakfast foods when the first customer walked into the store. The man nodded as he pushed through the door.

"Two poppy-seed bagels and a large coffee," said the man. Jacob recognized the look of automation and resignation in the man's eyes. Jacob brought the bagels over to the wrapping counter and caught a glimpse of himself in a pie server. His own eyes looked excited and bright. He placed the bagels in a bag and handed them over.

"Coffee?" asked the man.

Jacob realized he hadn't made any coffee. The baker didn't mention it and he didn't remember seeing a coffee maker anywhere in the shop. "I don't think I have coffee," said Jacob.

"You don't think? You don't know whether or not you have coffee?" asked the man.

"I mean our supplier didn't show up this morning. Sorry," said Jacob.

"Guess I'll have to live with the machine at the train station," replied the man. "How much?"

Jacob paused. He'd never asked the baker how much to charge for anything. "Two dollars," he said finally.

"Here you go," said the man handing him two crumbled dollars. He hurried out of the store.

Jacob put the money into the register. It took a moment for him to understand he'd made his first sale. He smiled. "Tomorrow I'll have coffee," he said to himself.

Jacob had four additional customers through the morning. Looking at the remaining number of bagels and muffins he was somewhat disappointed. He supposed it wasn't bad for simply washing the windows and unlocking the front doors. But Jacob knew enough about cost and revenue to understand they hadn't covered the day's expenses. He'd have to do better.

Late in the morning Jacob heard the bells from the front door ring as he was preparing the afternoon's cakes and cookies. He went out into the front of the shop. It was the same policeman he'd seen the day he couldn't find the bakery.

"Morning," said the policeman.

"Good morning," said Jacob.

"Any coffee?" asked the policeman. "Stuff at the station is pretty bad."

"My supplier didn't show up this morning," answered Jacob. He'd answered this question five other times today. "We'll definitely have coffee tomorrow."

"And a new supplier, I imagine," said the policeman making conversation.

"Yes," said Jacob. Actually he was planning to run to the supermarket on the highway and bring the coffeemaker from his home.

"A new business can be tough," said the policeman. "You don't know who you can count on."

Jacob was puzzled. He was under the impression the bakery had been here for many years. "Hasn't there always been a bakery here?"

"This building has been a bakery as long as I remember," said the policeman. "But today's the first day I've seen it open in a long time. So you just work here, then?"

"Yes," said Jacob. "I started a couple of weeks ago."

"Welcome to the neighborhood," said the policeman. He shook Jacob's hand. "I'm Officer Ted Chambers. The kids around town call me Officer Ted." The policeman ran his fingers through his receding hairline. "It makes me feel old, actually."

"Officer Chambers, then" said Jacob.

"Ted should be fine," said the policeman. "How fresh are the muffins?"

"Made this morning," said Jacob with pride. "The banana cranberry's good."

"I'll have one of those," said Ted.

Jacob took the muffin out and wrapped it.

"How much do I owe you?" asked Ted.

"On the house," said Jacob. He remembered someone telling him once it was a good idea to allow the police and fireman to eat free. "I was getting ready to take them over to the church anyway."

"Giving away the leftovers," said Ted. "Good for you." He took the muffin from Jacob. "I'll spread the word around town you're open. Just make sure you have coffee tomorrow."

"Definitely," said Jacob.

At the end of the day Jacob totaled the day's receipts before cleaning up. "We didn't sell much today," said Jacob to the baker as he was gathering up the day's leftovers.

"What did you sell?" asked the baker.

"About a dozen and a half bagels, seven muffins and two pies," answered Jacob. "I have four cakes leftover."

"Sounds like a good first day to me," said the baker. "My first day I sold only three danish."

"We didn't make enough to cover the expenses," said Jacob.

"It's good that you're keeping track of the receipts day to day," said the baker. "But as long as everything balances by the end of the month you'll be fine."

Jacob was still skeptical but he decided to let it go for now. "The money is in the register," he said.

"Your money is in the register," said the baker. "You keep what you earn." Jacob started to protest but the baker shook his head.

"Thank you,' said Jacob.

"Thank you," replied the baker. "Now run your errands and get some rest. Tomorrow will be busier."

12.

The baker was right. The next day was busier. Within the first hour of unlocking the door Jacob had already served twice as many customers. The coffee was a hit. Tomorrow he decided he would start serving tea as well. A couple of the new customers asked for it.

Another customer inquired about cakes and pies. Jacob explained he made those later in the day. She said she would stop back, especially if he could make a cherry. Jacob resolved to have at least a limited selection of cakes, cookies and pies out in the morning.

Jacob had a renewed hope for the bakery. He still wasn't on track to cover all the expenses but he'd done much better. He also had several ideas to continue improving things.

Near the end of the early morning rush Ted returned. "Coffee today?" he asked.

"Surely," said Jacob. He poured the officer a cup. "Fresh brewed," he said as he handed it over.

"Smells like it," said Ted. He took a sip. "Tastes like the brand my wife buys," he said.

"Probably is," said Jacob. "I picked it up last night at the supermarket."

Ted laughed and shook his head. "You do what you have to," said the policeman. "I admire your tenacity."

"Muffin today?" asked Jacob.

"Not today," said Ted patting his mid-section. "I had one of those breakfast bars. You should consider selling them here."

"Good idea," said Jacob.

"How much for the coffee?" asked Ted.

"Your money's no good here," said Jacob. "In fact I'm glad you stopped by. Would you mind taking some bagels over to the police station and firehouse for me? I thought it would be a neighborly gesture."

"And good business," said Ted with a wink.

"That too,' said Jacob. "I'd like to make it a daily thing."

"I'll talk to the fire chief," said Ted. "He has a young guy who runs errands in the morning. I'll have him stop over and pick them up every day. Put some flyers in there."

"Thanks," said Jacob.

"You'll have to work on the coffee, though," said Ted as he was leaving.

"I'm on it," said Jacob. "And the breakfast bars."

Ted waved his hand above his head as he walked out of the store with the extra bagels. Jacob took advantage of the lull in customers to wipe down the counters and straighten up the shelves.

"Morning," called out a cheery woman's voice as he was arranging some braided loaves.

"Good morning," said Jacob turning toward the door. A jovial looking woman came up the center isle.

"Marlene Holiday," announced the woman. "I own the flower shop on the next block. I smelled your wonderful creations and just had to come over."

"Thank you," said Jacob. "Can I offer you a bagel or a muffin?"

"Oh I don't fool around with warm up sweets," said Marlene with a wide smile. "Cut me a piece of that nice apple pie."

Jacob cut a generous piece of pie and served it to Marlene. They sat down around the tall table in the corner of the shop. "Coffee?" he asked.

"Yes, please," said Marlene. "Won't you join me in a piece?"

Jacob considered apple pie a bit too rich for breakfast. "I sample as I bake," he said. "I'm usually pretty full by this time of the morning."

"There's always room for pie," said Marlene as she forked a large hunk into her mouth. "Heavenly."

"Thank you," said Jacob pouring the coffee. "I will join you in a cup of coffee." He glanced at the door.

"Don't worry," said Marlene. "The trains run twenty minutes apart. People have their morning timed pretty well, including their coffee stop."

"I'm still learning the schedules," said Jacob. "It's my second day."

"You seem to be doing fine," said Marlene. "I saw you sent bagels to the police and fire stations – a good move. I make sure they always have fresh flower arrangements."

"How long have you owned the flower shop?" asked Jacob.

"Almost twenty years," said Marlene. "There were a lot more businesses here in town then."

"What happened?" asked Jacob.

"Most places moved out to the highway," answered Marlene. "More traffic there, I guess."

"That's too bad," said Jacob. "I like it here."

"I'll have to introduce you to the other shopkeepers," said Marlene. "Besides my flower shop, the travel agency is still open. There's also the used record store, newspaper agency, the shoe store and, of course, the furniture store."

"What about the two restaurants?" asked Jacob.

"The restaurants change hands a lot," replied Marlene. "We never get to know the owners very well."

"They never seem to be very good," admitted Jacob.

"I know," said Marlene. She finished the last bite of her pie. "If you want I can bring some flowers over to dress the place up a bit. No charge, of course."

"Thank you," said Jacob. "I'll supply the pie and coffee."

"You keep baking pies like that," said Marlene gesturing to her now empty plate, "and I'll bring you flowers every day."

Marlene gave Jacob's hand a brisk shake and left. Jacob gathered up her plate and fork and took it quickly to the kitchen. According to Marlene he could expect another rush in a few minutes.

Jacob removed the last of the bagels and muffins from the case to make room for the afternoon sweets. He was just about to go back into the kitchen when a young woman walked into the shop. She wore blue pants and a starched uniform shirt with a badge. Her face looked familiar.

"Hello," she said. "I'm deputy chief Samuels. I mean Kate Samuels. I'm with the fire department. I just wanted to come over and thank..." she trailed off.

Jacob suddenly realized she was the young woman he'd met over two weeks ago at the bookstore. "I like art," he said with a smile.

"It's amazing how much better that line works now," said Kate.

"I'm Jacob," he replied.

"It's nice to meet you...and thank you for the bagels," said Kate.

"You're welcome," said Jacob. "Did Ted ask about sending someone over?"

"Yes," said Kate. "We'll send Bobby over in the morning. He's a good kid - wants to be a fireman. Chief wants him to get his GED first."

"I'd send over coffee," said Jacob. "But I'm having trouble with my supplier."

"That's okay," said Kate. "We make our own. The bagels are more than enough. So when did you start working at the bakery?"

"The day we met in the bookstore," answered Jacob.

"That's why you had the book on food still life," said Kate.

"Looking for inspiration, I guess," said Jacob.

"It must have worked," said Kate. "The bagels were delicious."

"Thank you," said Jacob with a slight blush.

"I'd better get back to the station," said Kate. "Thanks again for breakfast."

"Anytime," said Jacob. He knew he should say something more but couldn't think of anything. He didn't want to end on another bad line. Kate paused for a moment and gave him a smile before leaving the bakery.

The baker poked his head out from the kitchen. "There's always more to learn," he said.

13.

By the fourth day Jacob had established an even rhythm between baking and serving customers. He'd also found a coffee and tea supplier. Everything seemed to be falling into place. "Everything except the glass display case," said Jacob.

"Still haven't found your best creation?" asked the baker.

"No," replied Jacob. He looked in the display case. It held an assortment of cakes, pastries and cookies. They all looked appetizing enough, but Jacob didn't consider any of them a specialty.

"What does your heart tell you?" asked the baker.

Jacob paused for a moment. He scanned his feelings regarding the various items he'd learned to make. Jacob liked baking pies but didn't find anything special about the pies he made. His cookies were standard fare: sugar, chocolate chip and peanut butter. Cakes were some of his best work. He liked to combine flavors.

"Anything?" prompted the baker.

"Cakes?" suggested Jacob.

"You don't sound convinced," said the baker with a short chuckle. "You'll know your special item when you make it."

"I suppose," said Jacob. "You'd think I'd at least have an idea."

"The evening rush is probably over," said the baker. "Why don't you close up for the day?"

"I'll close up," said Jacob, "but I think I'll stay around and practice for awhile."

"Good for you," said the baker. "I'll see you tomorrow."

Jacob flipped the sign on the front door to "closed" and went into the kitchen. He busied himself by cleaning up for awhile. While cleaning he tried to remember the ivy design on the pies in his earlier dream. After he was finished he took some fresh dough from the refrigerator. Jacob rolled out the dough and cut it into several strips.

He tried to make the shapes necessary to create the ivy. No matter how careful he was, the branches always seemed to come out wrong. The designs barely resembled the ones he remembered. Eventually he gave up and balled all the dough back together. He added some spices and re-rolled the dough. Using a star-shaped cookie cutter he made a tray of cookies.

The cookies didn't take long to bake; the oven was still warm from the day. The batch was good, although Jacob thought he'd added a little too much nutmeg. There was nothing really special about the cookies, though. Jacob packed the cookies in tins and placed them in the front of the shop for sale the next day.

Next he baked a cake. It was raspberry and dark chocolate, a recipe he'd improvised. The cake was very good and Jacob didn't know of anything quite like it. Still, it didn't feel like a signature item. He decided to take the cake to Marlene and ask her what she thought.

Jacob shut off the oven and closed up for the day. He walked out of the store with the wrapped cake under his arm and locked the front door. He started to walk towards the flower store when he heard a familiar voice.

"Anything good?" asked Kate.

"Oh, this?" said Jacob. "It's an extra cake. I thought I'd take it down to Marlene at the flower store."

"She'll appreciate that," said Kate. "How is business?"

"Good," said Jacob. "The crowds pick up every day."

"I'm glad," said Kate. "Did you find a way to work in any art yet?" she said with a smile.

"Not yet," said Jacob. "But I'll let you know when I do."

"I hope so," said Kate. "Have a good night."

"You too," replied Jacob. He watched as she walked to the end of the street. After she disappeared around the corner he continued to the flower shop. Marlene wasn't there so Jacob left the cake with one of her workers. The worker put the cake in one of the flower refrigerators. It looked odd in with the daisies and roses but at least it would keep.

On the way home he thought more about Kate. Jacob wondered how long she'd been a member of the fire company. He'd never noticed her in town before.

Jacob decided to take the longer route home and forced himself to walk slower. He was surprised to see the number of people around. Downtown people shuffled in and out of the few shops still open. People stared at the destination posters in the travel store windows and considered the latest styles on display in the shoe store. Most were kind enough to nod at Jacob as he walked past.

A couple of people were headed into side doors leading to the apartments above the stores. He remembered staring up at those windows as a child and making up stories about each one. "A pet doctor lives there," he'd say to his mother as they walked through town to buy new shoes or pick up the newspaper.

"Really?" said his mother. "Who lives in that one?"

"I bet the mailman lives there," said Jacob.

"How do you know?" asked his mother.

"Because the curtains are blue," replied Jacob with complete confidence.

He always imagined people with simple jobs that were easy to understand. A pet doctor helped sick animals. The mailman delivered letters. As an adult he'd discovered there weren't many simple jobs anymore.

"What do you do again, dear?" his mother asked a few weeks ago.

"I'm in process improvement," replied Jacob.

"Okay," said his mother. "I understand."

Jacob could tell she didn't. "I figure out how we can do things better," he added.

"But what does your company make?" asked his mother.

"We don't make anything," replied Jacob. It occurred to him that a lot of companies didn't seem to make anything these days. "We help the companies that make things."

"So you help them make things better," concluded his mother.

"Not exactly," said Jacob. "We help them find other companies to help them make things better."

"Oh," said his mother.

Jacob started to reply but he wasn't sure if he understood it either. He had that conversation just three days before he finally ran away from his job. Jacob didn't tell his parents about the change yet. The next time he spoke to his mother, though, he'd be happy to tell her he was a baker.

Still looking at the windows, Jacob was amazed at the thought of all those individual people. They all had families, jobs and hobbies. Each was unique – almost like a batch of cookies. Even when the cookies came from the same batch each one looked and tasted a bit different. He chuckled at the idea.

"Good joke?" asked a voice to his right.

Jacob looked over and saw a man who came into the bakery almost every morning. "No," replied Jacob. "I was just thinking people are like cookies."

"A baker and a philosopher," said the man. "See you tomorrow morning." The man continued up his walk and into his house. Jacob gave him a wave and a smile.

Jacob continued on his way and watched over people as they mowed their lawns and played with their children. He suddenly felt a little alone. He realized he'd mainly focused on work for the past few years.

Jacob's parents had retired and moved away and he'd bought their house. It had been a long time since he'd actually looked at the town, though. At some point he'd just started passing through on his way to something or somewhere else.

As he got older he thought less and less about the stories behind each door and window. After awhile he'd stopped thinking about even his own story. Then one day he ran home. That's when his story started to get interesting again. And he started to be interested in other people's stories again.

14.

"You're over-baking those cookies," said the baker. "People like them a little doughy."

"I know," said Jacob. "I haven't found the right rotation for them in the oven yet. It's more difficult because they're smaller."

"Then why not make them bigger?" suggested the baker.

"The recipe says to make them two inches in diameter," said Jacob.

"Then change it," replied the baker. "Always make things the appropriate size. If the cookies need to be a bit bigger, make them bigger."

Jacob nodded and continued working. He was making several braided rolls for the evening rush. The rolls were popular additions for dinner. The baker looked over his shoulder for a moment.

"Good braids," said the baker. "They are just right. Not too tight and not too loose."

"How did you start baking?" asked Jacob while he continued to work.

"I found a bunch of recipes in the drawer of an old desk," replied the baker. "I'd left home a week earlier to make my own way. I read through the recipes and knew then I wanted to be a baker."

"Who wrote the recipes?" asked Jacob.

"I never found out," said the baker. "But it wasn't important. I learned from those recipes – just as you are learning from me. Some day another baker will learn from you."

"Don't you want to know who wrote the recipes or why they were in the desk?" asked Jacob.

"Sometimes a thing is more magical when you don't know everything about it," said the baker. "Before I found the recipes I was unsure of my purpose in life. After reading them I knew. That was magical."

Jacob considered this. "I think baking is magical," he said.

"I thought you might," said the baker.

Later in the day Jacob had Marlene over for cake and coffee. Jacob wanted to try out a new cake recipe on her. It might even be an item for the display case.

"So what do you think?" asked Jacob. Marlene took a final bite of cake and washed it down with a gulp of coffee.

"Very good," replied Marlene.

"But is it a signature dessert?" asked Jacob.

"I'm not sure," said Marlene. "You've been giving me different desserts to try for almost two weeks now. What are we looking for again?"

"What to put in there," said Jacob, pointing to the glass display case.

"I think that's something you need to decide," said Marlene. "But I appreciate all the desserts."

"Don't you have a flower arrangement that's unique to your shop?" asked Jacob.

Marlene was quiet for a moment. "I never really thought about it," she said. "I suppose I'm fond of certain plants and accents."

Jacob slumped down on the stool opposite Marlene. "The baker said I should find my own signature creation. Something special for the glass display case."

"Maybe you're rushing things," suggested Marlene.

Jacob thought about this. His previous work always involved deadlines. A report had to be in by a certain date. A project had to be completed by the end of the quarter. Faster was almost always better. Things were never done soon enough. Jacob looked around the bakery and realized he'd been doing the same thing here.

He was impatient to finish cleaning and move on to baking. He had worked all night to get better at making the dough. He wanted to clean the windows before they had any bread or cakes out. He wanted to find a specialty when there were hundreds of things he'd never baked.

"I guess I have been moving too fast," said Jacob. "My last job was always hurried."

"You've certainly taken the bakery far in a short amount of time," agreed Marlene. "You've had some good ideas and have a number of steady customers. Many new businesses never even get off the ground – especially around here."

"So am I doing the right thing?" asked Jacob.

"I think you're doing well with the business," answered Marlene. "But I think you're rushing your creativity away. Take time to enjoy what you're doing."

"Now you're starting to sound like the baker," said Jacob.

"I think the baker is a wise man," said Marlene.

The bell over the door rang and Kate entered carrying a bouquet of flowers. She gave Jacob a hug. "Thank you so much," she said. "They're beautiful."

Jacob wasn't sure what to say. "I...." he stammered.

"Why Jacob you sly dog," interjected Marlene. She gave him a wink. "Sending flowers to Kate – and so pretty. How did you know daisies are her favorite?"

"Don't play coy, Marlene," said Kate. "You must have told him they were my favorite. The flowers came from your shop. I recognize your arrangement style."

"I guess I do have a signature arrangement," said Marlene. She gave Jacob another wink.

"I think dinner is a great idea," said Kate, "as long as you let me cook."

Jacob was confused again. Marlene came to his rescue. "He was worried about being so forward," said Marlene. "But I told him you preferred men who were a little bold."

Kate blushed. "Marlene..." she protested. She turned back to Jacob. "How about tomorrow night?"

"Tomorrow isn't good," replied Marlene. "I'm introducing Jacob to the shop owners tomorrow night."

"That's a good idea," said Kate. "You'll actually like some of them," she said ominously. "Can you make it the night after?"

"Sure," said Jacob. He decided it was time he spoke up for himself.

"Great," said Kate. "I'll expect you to bring dessert, of course."

"Of course," said Jacob.

Kate gave him another smile and shuffled back out the door. Jacob stared after her for a minute before looking at Marlene. "What was that all about?" he asked.

"I just thought you two needed a little push," replied Marlene. "I saw her come out of the bakery a couple of times. And I've seen you chatting with her on the street."

"I was doing okay," protested Jacob.

"You were taking forever," said Marlene.

"A minute ago you told me not to rush," replied Jacob.

"That was advice about baking and business," said Marlene. "You should never delay the heart." Marlene finished the rest of her coffee. "I'd better get back to the shop. You're welcome, by the way."

"Thank you, Marlene," said Jacob.

15.

Jacob was uneasy as he walked to the front door. He liked Marlene but didn't know what to expect of the other shop owners in town. He couldn't recall seeing any of them except the owner of the furniture store. Jacob's parents had gone there several times to buy furniture when he was still young.

He always remembered the storeowner as extremely tall and extremely scary. He only tolerated children in the store and always stared at Jacob while his parents shopped. He was just waiting for Jacob to make something dirty or knock something over. One time Jacob was bold enough to say he liked a certain chair in the store. The owner gave him a frown and asked if he'd be paying cash or charge.

Jacob rang the bell on the front door and heard a series of chimes in the background. The door swung open and Jacob found himself staring at the chest of a tall man clad in a drab blue suit. He looked up into the man's face. The man stared down at him with familiar sunken eyes. Jacob felt the hair on his arms stand on end. It was the furniture storeowner.

"Hello Jacob," said the man in a deep, monotone voice. "Please come in and try not to knock anything over."

"Oh don't be so stodgy," said a woman from behind him. "Besides, it's my house." The woman pushed him aside and introduced herself. "Sofia Mendez. I own the travel agency. It looks like you've already met Marlow."

Sofia was a smartly dressed woman in her mid-forties. She was not unattractive, although Jacob thought she was wearing too much make-up. She appeared to be engaged in a full assault against middle age.

"Hello," said Jacob shaking her hand. The woman led him into the house and began pointing out the various features. "The main foyer is hardwood imported from Germany. This wallpaper was illustrated by hand in Italy. I got the statue on the mantle there from Romania. Have you ever visited there?"

"No," said Jacob. "I haven't traveled much."

"We'll have to change that," said Sofia.

"I'd stay put if I were you, young man," said a small man sitting on a couch in the next room. He wore a rumpled suit and large, round glasses. "Nothing but inconvenience when you travel. Stay at home where it's comfortable."

"Like an old pair of shoes," said Marlene sitting down next to him. "Right Carson?"

"Comfort is the most important quality in a shoe," answered Carson.

"You must be the shoe store owner," said Jacob extending his hand. The man got part way up and shook his hand. "John Carson. Carson's shoes."

"Nice to meet you," said Jacob.

"Please sit down," said Sofia. "Can I get you something to drink?"

"Do you have any iced tea?" asked Jacob taking a seat opposite Marlene and Carson.

"Just a minute," said Sofia leaving the room. "Chapal and the Moores should be here soon."

Marlow squeezed himself into a mission-style chair much too small for him. "I sold her this chair," said Marlow with pride. "Best piece of furniture in the house - handcrafted in the Midwest."

"Sofia has filled this whole house with wonderful things from all over the world and you like a chair from Ohio," said Marlene.

"Who are Chapal and the Moores?" asked Jacob to change the subject.

"Chapal owns the news agency now," answered Carson. "The Moores have the used record store downtown. I have no idea how they manage to stay in business."

"They rely on the traffic as people come to my furniture store," said Marlow.

"We all pick up traffic from each other," corrected Marlene.

"Some of us more than others," replied Marlow.

"Are we squabbling again?" asked Sofia as she came back into the room with Jacob's iced tea.

"Welcome to the neighborhood," said Marlene.

"Thanks," said Jacob.

The doorbell rang. "That must be more of the guests," said Sofia on her way to the door.

Jacob heard voices in the foyer and Sofia re-emerged with an Indian man around his age. "Jacob, this is Chapal."

Jacob stood up and shook Chapal's hand. He was surprised by Chapal's young age. "Nice to meet you," he stammered.

"Hello," said Chapal. "Is something wrong?"

"No," replied Jacob. "I'm just surprised at how young you are."

"I think he just called the rest of us old," interjected Carson.

"I meant I'm impressed he owns a store at his age," said Jacob.

"Thank you," said Chapal. "But don't you own a store as well?"

"I'm just a baker," said Jacob.

"As long as you know who you are," replied Chapal, "that is the important thing."

"Staying in business is the most important thing," corrected Marlow. "And that is becoming increasingly more difficult."

"So what are we going to do about it?" asked Chapal. "You always give us gloomy predictions, but you never have any ideas."

"My store has been in town the longest and it is the largest," replied Marlow. He crossed his arms. "It is the main reason people come into town."

"We're not going to come up with any ideas by fighting about it," said Carson.

"Carson's right," agreed Marlene. "Let's get started. Like usual we'll go around the room and everyone has to give at least one idea."

"Agreed," said Chapal sitting down.

"Shouldn't we wait until the Moores arrive?" asked Carson.

"The Moores are always late," replied Chapal. "Let's just get started. I suggest we develop a book of coupons valid at all the businesses in town. We can put them in the local newspaper. The paper has several new advertising incentives right now..."

"Margins in the furniture business are very close," snapped Marlow. "I can't be offering discounts."

The doorbell rang again and Sofia went to the door. She returned with a middle aged couple wearing jeans, concert t-shirts and tattered leather jackets. Jacob presumed they were the Moores.

"Jacob, this is Howie and Carly Moore," said Sofia. "I believe you two know everyone else." Howie and Carly greeted everyone before sitting down on a love seat. "We were just going over some ideas," explained Sofia.

"And Marlow was probably shooting them all down," said Howie.

"It's not as though anyone ever listens," said Marlow. "Jacob, don't you think that glass is too close to the edge of the table?"

Jacob looked down at his drink. It was about an inch from the edge so he slid it further onto the table. "Maybe we should continue going around with ideas," he suggested.

"I believe Carson is next," added Marlene. "Go ahead Carson."

"I suggest we draft a request to the town council," said Marlow.

"Not the bureaucrats!" protested Howie.

"Now who's the one shooting down ideas?" said Marlow smugly.

"This squabbling is not getting us more customers," said Chapal.

"Chapal's right," added Carly. "What about a community art project? We could all paint a mural."

"We'd definitely need to talk to the town council about that," said Carson.

"I've spoken to the town council members on several occasions," said Sofia. "They're not very helpful."

This launched the group into a discussion about the town council. Jacob sat back and listened. He never realized there was so much drama in the small town. It reminded him of his thoughts about the people behind all the windows.

The meeting broke up a couple of hours later. Howie and Carly had to get home to take care of their children and Carson had an early shipment arriving in the morning. No one ever got back to ideas. Jacob left with the impression most of the meetings went the same way.

16.

"Now taste this one," said Freda as she handed him a freshly cut piece of fruit. Jacob had learned in subsequent visits that the fruit distributor business had been in Freda's family for years. She had practically grown up picking out fruit.

Jacob took a bite of the mango. "It's very sweet," he said. "Like it's trying hard to gain your approval."

"And?" prompted Freda.

Jacob took another bite. He chewed longer this time and allowed the fibers to churn around in his mouth. Jacob knew Freda wanted him to detect something else. He finally gave up and swallowed the fruit. "I'm not sure," said Jacob.

"You should be able to detect an underlying acidity in the taste," said Freda.

"Oh," said Jacob. As soon as Freda said the words he could detect a faint echo of the citrus acid on his palette. "I know how to use the effect of the acidity when I bake," he added.

"I know," said Freda. "I've tasted your mango tarts. But you'll be even better if you can taste those elements in the raw ingredients."

"I guess I have a lot to learn," said Jacob. Sometimes he felt like there was too much he didn't know.

"Yes," replied Freda, "but you should be excited about it. I'd love to be able to experience all these tastes for the first time again. Enjoy it while you can."

Jacob ate a bit more of the mango and swished it around in his mouth. He allowed the juices to soak into his tongue and palette. Finally he swallowed. "I think there's a small bite underneath the sweetness."

"Good," said Freda. "Let's try another one." She cut up a papaya and handed him a piece.

"It's sweet and light," said Jacob. "It knows it's good, but it's still a bit shy."

"What makes it different from the mango?" asked Freda.

"It's less sweet," said Jacob, focusing on the taste.

"What else?" asked Freda.

Jacob took another bite. He chewed the fruit for a moment and swallowed. He still had no ideas. Jacob looked at Freda for guidance.

"What about the texture?" prompted Freda.

Jacob's eyes widened. He understood in an instant. "It was denser," he said. "The mango was made up of individual fibers. I could feel them when I chewed."

"Now you've got it," said Freda.

"Textures hold flavor in different ways," added Jacob.

"That's right," replied Freda. "It also affects the visceral experience of eating the fruit. Biting into a drupe is not the same experience as biting into an aggregate."

Jacob recalled the baker explaining a drupe was a single fruit, characterized by a fleshy outside, hard middle and a seed. Mangos, peaches and plums were all drupes. Aggregates consisted of a cluster of several fruits produced from a single flower. Blackberries, raspberries and strawberries were aggregates.

"Do your think that changes the taste itself?" Jacob asked.

Freda considered the question for a moment. "When you bite into the hard inside of the drupe, the taste is slow and steady."

"When you bite into an aggregate," added Jacob, "the flavor rushes into your mouth almost like a liquid."

"With really ripe fruit it bursts into your mouth as you break the skin," agreed Freda.

Jacob nodded.

"Have you worked with multiple fruits yet?" asked Freda.

"Just pineapple and fig," replied Jacob. He found the concept of multiple fruits odd and sometimes contradictory. They were a cluster of fruits like aggregates, but developed form multiple flowers. Some multiples like pineapple grew in large clusters, others were more like mini-drupes.

"Multiples can be interesting," continued Freda. "Each one has its own characteristics."

"I know," said Jacob.

"Is that frustration I detect?" replied Freda.

"Sometimes it's difficult to combine the tastes and textures," said Jacob. "What works with a peach will usually work with a mango. Most berries react in similar ways, even though they produce different tastes."

"But every multiple seems to act a little different," said Freda.

"That's right," agreed Jacob.

"Wait until the next time I get some mulberries in," said Freda. "They'll win you over to multiple fruits." She picked up a piece of the mango and bit into it.

"Nothing compares to biting into a fruit for the first time," said Freda. "Every time I eat a fruit I've already had it's like capturing a little of that memory of the first taste."

"I never thought of it that way," said Jacob. "Thanks for the fruit...and the lesson. I'd better get over to the dairy. I need to set up regular deliveries with them."

"You're still picking up your milk and eggs?" asked Freda.

"Yes," replied Jacob. "Hopefully not after today."

Jacob left the fruit distributor and drove to the dairy. It was relatively quiet when he arrived. By stopping at the fruit vender first he had avoided the rush. Pre-ordering dairy products presented a new challenge for Jacob. Unlike flour and spices, milk and eggs did not keep for an extended amount of time. Even fruit could be put up as preserves if he bought too much.

After the initial list of supplies, the baker had been vague about the amount of ingredients they should keep in stock. Jacob had the impression it was important he figure it out on his own. Jacob's plan was to consult with the manager at the dairy. Almost as soon as Jacob got out of the truck an older man approached him.

"Can I help you with anything?" asked the man. He set down a pail of feed he'd been carrying and wiped his hands on an old rag he took from his shirt pocket. Both his hands and face were dry and cracked. Jacob thought the man looked over-used.

"I need to arrange for daily milk delivery," said Jacob.

"We don't do home deliveries," answered the man. "You can buy gallons or half gallons in the store." He gestured towards a small barn that had been converted to retail store and ice cream parlor.

"It's for a bakery," said Jacob.

"Why didn't you say so?" grumbled the man. "Go to the store counter and ask for Sally. She'll set you up."

The man started to walk away but Jacob stopped him. "Can I ask you a question?" The man reluctantly put his pail down and turned back to Jacob. Jacob thought he'd never meet anyone less pleasant than Marlow but this man offered the possibility.

"I could use some help deciding how much to order," said Jacob.

The already cavernous scow on the man's face deepened even further. "How would I know how much milk you need?" The man stalked away, spilling some of the feed out of the pail as he went. Several small birds landed and began to peck at the feed on the ground.

Jacob watched the birds and realized the man was right – even if he was overly harsh about it. How could he know how much milk the bakery needed? That was for Jacob to figure out.

The birds finished eating the fallen seed and flew away. This gave Jacob an idea: maybe he was just over thinking the problem. The man with the pail had spilled a bit of seed on the ground, but it hadn't gone to waste. The wild birds ate the seed. The problem of milk delivery might not be how to get the order exactly right, but how to deal with anything left over.

The problem seemed complex but was actually simply when Jacob looked at it the right way. He totaled a daily estimate of milk, cream and eggs in his head while he walked towards the small converted barn. By the time he'd reached the door Jacob had already thought of several uses for the leftover dairy products.

17.

"How was the meeting?" called Kate from the kitchen.

"Interesting," replied Jacob. He was staring at a wall of pictures in the living room of Kate's apartment. She actually lived in one of the apartments above the stores downtown – the furniture store as a matter of fact. Jacob was finally getting to see the world behind one of the windows.

"Is that all?" asked Kate.

"Everyone seemed friendly," replied Jacob, "except for the furniture store owner. He still scares me after all these years."

"At least he's not your landlord," replied Kate.

"True," said Jacob. He walked into the kitchen. "Can I help?" he asked.

"Thanks," replied Kate. "I'm fine. What kind of pie did you bake?"

"One of the baker's recipes," replied Jacob. "It's a combination of berries and spices."

"How did you start working for the baker?" asked Kate while chopping some carrots. "I didn't even know the shop was open."

Jacob thought about where to start and decided to tell her the whole story. "I was sitting at my old job one day and realized I just didn't like it," said Jacob. "So I got up and left."

"You mean you quit?" asked Kate.

"No I just left. Walked out – practically ran out. I rode the train home and started to run from the station back to the house. That's the first time I met the baker. He was sweeping outside of his shop."

"This was before we met at the bookstore?" asked Kate.

"The day before," replied Jacob. "I was running by and the baker called me the 'gingerbread man.'"

"Oh," said Kate. "Like the story. Because you were running."

Jacob tried to recall the story. "The baker mentioned something about a story too," he said.

"Run, run as fast as you can," said Kate. "You can't catch me because I'm the gingerbread man."

"I think I remember," replied Jacob.

"Watch the stove for a minute," said Kate. She went into the other room and after a few minutes returned with a children's book. "Here you go," she said. "I thought I had a copy."

Jacob looked at the cover. A gingerbread man was hopping out of an oven, much to the chagrin of an old woman. He started to look through it.

"You can keep it," said Kate going back to the stove. "Let's eat before it gets cold. You can finish telling me about the baker."

Kate put the dishes on the table and they sat down to eat. The main dish was pasta, accompanied by salad and bread. Jacob took a few bites before continuing with his story. "I didn't say much to the baker that first day, but I did walk back downtown hoping to see him again."

"How did you get a job as his apprentice?" asked Kate.

"It really just happened," answered Jacob. "He asked if I would sweep a bit for him. After I was finished he had me clean the shelves and displays. From there it was on to the kitchen. Within a few days I was baking bagels, breads and muffins. Now that I've learned the basics we've been working on more complex recipes."

"Did you want to be a baker?" asked Kate.

Jacob considered the question. "I didn't know I wanted to be a baker," he said.

"But you like it, right?" prompted Kate.

"I really do," replied Jacob.

"So what about the baker?" asked Kate. "How long has he had the shop in town?"

"I'm not sure," said Jacob. "I'd never noticed it before but it's easy to miss. One day..." Jacob trailed off. He took another bite of his salad.

"What is it?" asked Kate.

"This is going to sound odd," continued Jacob. "But one day I couldn't find the shop."

"You mean you wandered around before you found it," said Kate.

"No. I walked up and down the street several times," replied Jacob. "It's like the shop wasn't there."

"That doesn't make sense," said Kate.

"I know," said Jacob. "It's also odd you didn't notice the shop earlier. The firehouse is pretty close by."

"I was thinking that," confirmed Kate. "How long did you say he had the shop?"

"We don't really talk about his history much," said Jacob. "He told me the other day he'd learned how to bake from a set of old recipes he found in a desk. Now he's teaching me."

"Not every one likes to talk about themselves," replied Kate.

"I'm just happy to be learning a trade," said Jacob. "How long have you been with the fire department?"

"About six years," replied Kate. "Six years officially, but I've been hanging around the firehouse most of my life. My father and his father were fire fighters. My grandfather's retired. My father is the fire marshal for a county north of here."

"So it's a family tradition," said Jacob.

"Yes," replied Kate. "Although my father's a little surprised the girl in the family followed in his footsteps. Neither of my brothers was interested."

"What do they do?" asked Jacob.

"They both have corporate jobs," replied Kate. "I don't even understand what they do each day."

"I don't understand what I used to do either," agreed Jacob.

"You mean before you started baking," said Kate.

"That's right," said Jacob.

They ate in silence for a few moments. "Everything tastes great," said Jacob. "Thanks for cooking."

"You're welcome," said Kate. "Tell me more about your interest in art."

"I like art," said Jacob. "You already know that."

"What do you like about it?" asked Kate.

"I used to draw and paint when I was younger," answered Jacob. "I haven't done either in a long time."

"Why did you stop?" asked Kate.

"I wasn't that good," answered Jacob.

"That's no reason to stop," said Kate.

"You don't understand," said Jacob. "I really wasn't that good. After leaving my old job I looked through some of my art. It was much worse than I remembered: finger-painting on the side of the refrigerator bad."

"At least you're honest with yourself," said Kate.

"I am now," said Jacob. "I wasn't for a long time."

Jacob and Kate continued to talk as they finished the meal. Jacob discovered they actually had a lot in common. He was always skeptical about the idea of one right person for each person. However, he and Kate just seemed to fit. He felt comfortable and at ease, just like when he was at the bakery.

Kate cleared the table and suggested they sit in the living room for a while before dessert. 'I'd like to let my dinner settle a bit," said Kate. Jacob agreed and they sat down on the couch.

"I was thinking," continued Kate, "what if there was a way to combine your interest in art with your baking?"

"How do you mean?" asked Jacob.

"Remember the book you were buying the day we met in the bookstore?" asked Kate.

"Yes," said Jacob. "It was about paintings of food."

"What if food itself could be art?" suggested Kate. "In fact, maybe it is already. Who's to say there isn't art in that pie out there?"

"I never really thought about," said Jacob. "The baker used to put ivy designs on top of his pies."

"Exactly," agreed Kate. "You need to find a way to express your art through your baking."

Jacob paused. "I have no idea how to do that," he said.

"You don't need to figure it all out tonight," said Kate. "It's enough that you have the idea."

"All right," said Jacob. He sat back against the couch and thought about art and baking.

"This is the awkward pause," said Kate interrupting his musings.

"What?" asked Jacob.

"The awkward pause," repeated Kate, "when you're supposed to kiss me."

"Oh," said Jacob. "Now it's definitely awkward."

"Just kiss me," said Kate.

18.

Jacob stared at the smoking, gooey mess in the tray in front of him. Some sections were burnt to a crisp while others were still runny and raw. He poked at the mass with a spatula. This tray marked his tenth attempt at hand baking breakfast bars. On the counter were the dissected remains of several brands of store-bought bars. The grains were easy enough to figure out but Jacob was having difficulty with the substance holding it all together.

Jacob only made the mistake of suggesting they just buy the bars wholesale one time. The baker walked out of the room and did not return for the rest of the day. This was particularly problematic since Jacob was practicing a new cake recipe. Luckily he managed to figure it out on the third batch. The next day the baker suggested he figure out the breakfast bars the same way.

That same evening Jacob started trying to discover a recipe to make the bars. So far he had ruined fourteen baking trays in the process. He tried scraping away the burnt areas of the first tray but it was difficult to remove the charred grain from the metal. Jacob threw out the current tray and went to the cabinet for a fresh one.

Jacob decided to retire to the living room for a rest. He sat down on the couch and closed his eyes for a few minutes. When he opened them he saw the gingerbread man book from Kate. It was still on the coffee table from three nights ago. Jacob picked up the book and read through it.

"Run, run as fast as you can!" shouted the drawing of the defiant little cookie. "You can't catch me. I'm the Gingerbread Man."

Jacob flipped through the rest of the pages. After his escape from the oven the gingerbread man faced more of the same dangers. This animal or that animal would try to eat him. Each time he'd run away. Other than the running, Jacob still couldn't see the connection between himself and the gingerbread man. Perhaps the baker was reading a different version.

Jacob set the book back down and walked back into the kitchen. On the spur of the moment he went to the cabinet and got out molasses, cinnamon and ginger. Most of the other ingredients he would need were already out. Jacob rinsed out a bowl and creamed together a mixture of butter and sugar. He added an egg and molasses. Jacob set the bowl aside.

In a separate bowl he mixed flour, baking soda and salt with the ginger and cinnamon. He also added some ground cloves. Jacob blended the two mixtures together and put it in the refrigerator to chill. The oven was already pre-heated from his previous experiment with the breakfast bars so he went back into the living room to rest.

Jacob took a short nap on the couch. After he woke up he returned to the kitchen and removed the mixture from the refrigerator. He rolled out the batch and used a paring knife to cut the dough into the shapes of small men. He used a spatula to pick up the rest of the men and place them in a clean pan.

About ten minutes later the first batch of gingerbread men was ready. Contrary to the story, none of the little men hopped out of the oven and ran off. Jacob took a bite of one of the cookies while they were still warm. They were not bad, although a bit crisp. He decided to make the next batch a little thicker so they would come out softer.

In a sudden burst of inspiration he added some vanilla to the second batch. The addition added an interesting twist to the taste. Jacob also tweaked the amounts of ginger, cloves and molasses on the later batches. After a few more tries he had a tray of cookies he was satisfied enough with to take to the shop the next day.

"What do you think?" Jacob asked the group he'd gathered to sample the new cookies.

"Very good," said Marlene taking another bite of gingerbread.

"You like anything sweet," said Ted. "I think you've got a hit, though."

"Kate?" prompted Jacob.

"I like them too," replied Kate. She gave Jacob a peck on the cheek. "Looks like the book gave you some inspiration.

"I think it did," said Jacob. "Kate gave me a copy of the gingerbread man story the other night," he explained.

"You'll do well with these during the holidays," said Ted.

"I was going to add them to our daily stock," said Jacob feeling a bit dejected.

"Gingerbread all year round?" questioned Ted.
"It is a bit non-traditional," replied Marlene.

"The taste seems to go with winter," added Kate. "But I agree with Ted they'll fly off the shelves in late fall and winter."

"I don't think I said anything about flying off the shelves," said Ted. "I said he would do well."

After they left Jacob went into the kitchen to prepare for the afternoon rush. People usually began arriving on the four-thirty train. He liked to have the smell of bread drifting out of the shop by that time. The baker was in the corner looking over some sticky buns left over from the morning crowd.

"These are a little messy," said the baker.

"They are sticky buns," replied Jacob.

The baker just looked at him. Jacob had already learned the baker was not accustomed to dry humor. "They do look a bit runny," said Jacob.

"You need to balance the filling with the pastry better," said the baker. "These are Sunday pastries."

"I'm not sure I understand," said Jacob.

"On Sundays people relax with their breakfast," explained the baker. "They take their time and like to lick the cinnamon, nuts and icing from their fingers. During the week they're all in a hurry."

"They don't want to dwell on their food," said Jacob.

"Yes," confirmed the baker. "The world would be better if everyone savored their breakfast during the week."

"But we have a business to run," said Jacob.

"That's correct," said the baker. "During weekdays keep the flavor on the inside of the bread or pastry. During the weekends you can keep the flavor on the outside."

"I understand," said Jacob.

"Now let's see what you have here," said the baker. He walked over to tray of remaining gingerbread cookies. "What are these?"

"They're gingerbread men," answered Jacob. "I baked them at home last night."

The baker stared at the cookies and frowned. He put his hand to his chin. "These are not finished," he said.

"Everyone liked them," protested Jacob.

"I'm sure they tasted fine," said the baker. "But not all of food is in the taste."

Jacob sniffed the cookies. "They smell fine," he said.

"Do you have any icing left over from the sticky buns?" asked the baker.

"I think so," said Jacob. He went to the refrigerator and retrieved the remaining icing.

"Gingerbread men should have personality," explained the baker. Jacob looked over the cookies. Apparently the baker was not satisfied with the simple indentations he'd poked into them to indicate faces and buttons. Jacob squeezed the icing onto the first cookie and made the outline of a mouth. He gave the face two more dots for eyes and gave the body three buttons.

"Better?" asked Jacob.

"Much," replied the baker. "You have become a good baker is the last few weeks. You are good at the basics and have begun to experiment on your own. But you need to express yourself more in your creations."

"More decoration?" asked Jacob.

"Don't think of it as just decoration," replied the baker. "Think of it as art."

Back at home that night Jacob thought about what the baker had said. He did tend to focus on taste. Of course, he always iced his cakes evenly and took care that his cookies were round and consistent in size. However, he generally didn't decorate other than a few sprinkles of cinnamon or a dollop of whipped cream.

Jacob decided to make a few batches of cookies. While the dough was chilling he rummaged through his cabinets. A couple of years ago his parents had visited during the holidays. One night his mother suggested they make and decorate cookies. It was an activity they used to do frequently when Jacob was a child. Jacob was fairly sure he still had the collection of sprinkles, food coloring and other embellishments.

He located them in the back of the cabinet above the stove. Jacob set the items down on the counter and started to make a batch of icing. As he was whipping the mixture he had another idea. He called Kate and asked if she wanted to come over and decorate cookies.

By the time Kate arrived the dough was chilled enough for them to begin cutting out the cookies. "This batch is sugar cookies," said Jacob. "I thought we'd start simple."

They spent the next few hours decorating hundreds of cookies. After completing the sugar cookies they moved on to peanut butter cookies and eventually to Jacob's latest batch of gingerbread men. The results made his previous work seem drab in comparison. Jacob was sure they even tasted better.

19.

Jacob dragged the last table into place and rubbed the sweat off his forehead. He wasn't sure if outdoor tables would work but figured it was worth a try. Normally people bought and left. Today he was going to see if they would sit outside the shop and eat for a while. If it worked, people might buy more. At the very least it would attract more attention to the shop.

He looked at his watch. It wasn't yet eight o'clock. He scanned the street. Marlow watched him curiously from the adjacent corner of the intersection. He had evidently come from the newspaper agency. Jacob noticed he only bought the paper on Saturdays. Jacob gave Marlow a friendly wave. Marlow nodded in return. To Jacob's surprise he crossed the street and came over to the bakery.

This was the first time Jacob had ever seen Marlow cross to his side of the street. Usually he moved on a track between the furniture store and the newspaper store, the post office and the small deli where he often got his lunch. Jacob wiped his hands on his apron. He reached his hand out to Marlow.

Marlow looked down at Jacob's outstretched hand for a moment and then shifted his gaze to the tables. "Moving out already?" he asked.

"I thought people might want to eat outside," replied Jacob. "If it works I'll at least have the tables out on Saturday and Sunday."

"People are in such a hurry these days," said Marlow. "I'm surprised they stop to eat at all. Let alone sit here and eat."

"If people are in such a hurry," said Jacob, "why do they need furniture?"

Marlow gave him a scow. "Was that supposed to be humorous?" he asked.

"Yes?" said Jacob timidly. He couldn't imagine a time when Marlow wouldn't scare him.

"Witty," said Marlow. "Good luck with all this," he said, making a sweeping gesture over the tables. Marlow turned smartly and walked back to his furniture store.

"That guy gives me the willies," said Ted coming up from behind.

"He used to scare me when I was a kid," said Jacob. "I never grew out of it."

"Marlow lives near the house I grew up in," said Ted. "He was old then. We used to dare each other to run up and ring his doorbell."

"Anyone ever do it?" asked Jacob.

"Are you kidding?" asked Ted. "Tables look good anyway. Where did you find them?"

"Yard sale last week," said Jacob. "I spray painted them black."

"They came out good," said Ted. "I checked with the town council. If you want you can chain the tables on the side of the store when you're not using them. So you won't have to lug them in and out all the time."

"Thanks," said Jacob.

"You should take them in for the winter, though," said Ted.

"Right," replied Jacob.

Ted moved on and Jacob went back inside to continue getting ready. Customers began to trickle in around a half hour later. A few stayed to eat at the tables but the volume remained the same as most Saturdays and Sundays. People drove in to pick up bagels, muffins and cookies. Then they drove off.

"Nobody walks around anymore," said Carson later. He wandered in after the morning rush. Jacob offered him a cup of coffee and a bagel.

"Apparently," said Jacob.

"Marlow said you were trying a new idea," said Carson. "I thought I'd come down and take a look."

"How much traffic do you get during the weekends?" asked Jacob.

"It's a little busier on warm weekends," replied Carson. "Nice weather brings people out. I do most of my business just before the school year."

Jacob looked out the front windows. Slightly more people than usual were wandering around but the streets were generally empty.

"You're lucky," continued Carson. "At least people have reason to come here every day. People don't need shoes all that often – especially if they buy a good pair of shoes."

"Hello, gents," said Chapal as he entered the bakery. "The tables are a good idea, Jacob."

"Not many people have used them," replied Jacob.

"Not this week," replied Chapal. "You just need the people to see the tables this week. They'll sit in them next week."

"Always the optimist," added Carson.

"I'll try it for a few more weekends," said Jacob.

There was a noticeable change the following day. The tables were never completely full but they were never completely empty either. Even Marlow stopped for a cup of coffee and a plain bagel. Apparently Carson dragged him over. Marlene placed flower vases on each of the tables. Jacob was unsure when she did it but made a mental note to thank her.

At the end of the day Jacob gathered up the tables and chairs and chained them to the side of the bakery. He would set them out again next Saturday. In the meantime he continued to dwell on the number of people drawn to the stores downtown. It wasn't large enough to support many stores. But the lack of stores probably kept people away.

Jacob realized there were two types of stores surviving in town. The first type offered everyday staples such as the bakery, the newspaper store and the flower shop. The second type offered occasional necessities such as the travel agency, shoe store and furniture store. He thought about the Moores and supposed a rare or hard to find record also represented an occasional necessity.

He was a bit disheartened as he locked up for the day. The bakery was doing okay. He was paying his bills but he was skirting the edge. Jacob suspected the other businesses were doing the same.

The old question returned. What's the worst that could happen? Downtown traffic would eventually disappear. They would all have to shut down their businesses. They would be forced to work in places like the one Jacob had left.

Jacob made his way down to the flower shop with a plate of sugar cookies for Marlene. In truth, they were actually "half" sugar cookies. He had cut back the amount of sugar in the cookies and replaced it with a hint of lemon. Marlene seemed to eat a lot of desserts, especially since the bakery had re-opened.

Marlene greeted him at the door. "I can smell your baking from the corner," she said.

"I brought you some sugar cookies," said Jacob. "Thank you for the flowers on the tables."

"You're welcome," replied Marlene. She led him inside where one of her workers was putting an arrangement together. Jacob nodded to the woman but she ignored him and went about her work unhappily.

"How did it go?" asked Marlene.

"A little better today," said Jacob. "I'm going to keep putting the tables out for now."

"Good for you," said Marlene.

"Marlene," continued Jacob, "maybe we can get the merchants together again. I think we need to keep talking about ideas."

"Absolutely," replied Marlene enthusiastically. But then something caught her eye in the arrangement under construction. "Just a minute," she said. Marlene went over to the woman working on the arrangement.

"Sandy," began Marlene, "that's way too many lilies." Sandy looked annoyed.

"It's what the customer requested," said Sandy.

"They wanted lilies as the main flower, right?" asked Marlene.

"Yes," confirmed Sandy.

"It doesn't mean all the flowers in the arrangement have to be lilies," said Marlene. "That's not even an arrangement - just a bunch of lilies in a vase. You need to break it up," she continued. "Balance the lilies with other flowers."

"You need to cut the lilies with other flowers," added Jacob. "Like when we cut cream with milk or water."

"That's right," agreed Marlene.

"Marlene," said Jacob, "I have to go. I want to try something. Can you set up a meeting with the other shopkeepers?"

"I'll set up a meeting," said Marlene. "Go indulge your creativity."

"Thanks, Marlene," said Jacob as he ran out of the store.

Jacob ran all the way back to his house and straight into his kitchen. He immediately took out a bowl and began to combine butter and sugar. He mixed in eggs and molasses. Jacob only added half as much molasses as usual. He also only added half as much ginger. After a few minutes thought he added vanilla and a dash of cinnamon.

He added the dry ingredients and placed the mixture in the refrigerator to chill. Jacob turned the oven on to pre-heat and made some dinner. He ate and read from his books while he waited for the dough. Later when it had reached the correct temperature he rolled it out and cut out the shape of the cookies. He was able to taste the first batch about ten minutes later.

The recipe still needed work, but it was a step in the right direction. Jacob tasted a hint of gingerbread, but it was much lighter and airier. He called Kate to come over and sample for herself.

"I like it," said Kate about twenty minutes later. Jacob gave her a cookie from the second batch since they were fresh from the oven and still a bit warm. "It's like they have an echo of the holiday season."

"Do you think people would eat them year round?" asked Jacob.

"I would," said Kate. "They're not as over-powering as normal gingerbread cookies. But each bite has a taste of winter and the holidays. Eating them reminds me of tinsel and wrapping gifts."

"Good," said Jacob. "I'll try them out this week."

"Put out free samples," suggested Kate. "You'll have a hard time describing them if they're just sitting in the case."

"How do you know I'm putting them in the case?" asked Jacob.

"Just a hunch," replied Kate. When she kissed him, Jacob could taste a whisper of ginger on her lips. His heart told him she was right.

20.

"What do you call these?" asked one of the morning customers.

"Three season gingerbread," replied Jacob. "It's gingerbread for the rest of the year."

"When I eat these I think of making a fire on a cold night," said the customer.

"They remind me of decorating the tree," added another customer. "I'll take a dozen."

Jacob sold out of three season gingerbread cookies less than an hour after opening the store. After the morning rush he immediately began baking several more dozen for the evening crowd.

"Your new creation must be popular," said the baker as Jacob worked on several large batches. "Or perhaps you are eating them all yourself," joked the baker.

"They sold out pretty quick," confirmed Jacob.

"Excellent," said the baker. "Always find something unique you can offer people. For me it was the fruit and spice pies."

"Your recipes are very popular too," said Jacob.

"I was always good at mixing different ingredients to come up with something new," replied the baker. "You are good at seeing old things in a new way."

They were quiet for a while. Finally Jacob raised a new subject. "Did more people used to shop downtown?" he asked.

"There was a time everyone shopped downtown," replied the baker. "Those days have long passed."

"Do you think we can bring them back?" asked Jacob.

"That's not my question to answer," said the baker. "My job is to pass on my knowledge to you. That job is almost complete."

"If we keep losing people it won't matter," said Jacob.

"People always need bread," said the baker. "There's always a place for a baker."

"What about the others?" asked Jacob.

"As I said," replied the baker, "that's not my question to answer."

"I need to do something," said Jacob. He took out the first batch of three season gingerbread men and began to decorate them.

"You are good at seeing old things in a new way," said the baker.

Jacob looked down at the three-season ginger bread cookies and nodded. Later he had Marlene and Chapal over to try the cookies and talk about ideas. Chapal was impatient about the upcoming shopkeeper meeting.

"We should just have the meeting now," said Chapal. "The three of us are the only ones who do anything." Chapal gestured at Marlene and Jacob. They were sitting around the tall table in the corner of the bakery.

"That wouldn't be fair," replied Marlene.

"Marlow is always negative," said Chapal. "And Carson just wants to take everything to town council."

"What about Sofia and the Moores?" asked Jacob.

"Sofia travels too much," answered Chapal. "I'm not sure the Moores have any idea what's going on."

"I agree with Marlene," said Jacob. "It seems wrong to exclude anyone. We'd need everyone to cooperate anyway."

Marlene finished off another three-season gingerbread man. "These are absolutely wonderful," she said. "They remind me of pumpkin pie and candy canes."

"They are rather good," agreed Chapal. "How are they selling?"

"I've sold several batches every day since I introduced them last week," replied Jacob.

"Good for you, Jacob," said Chapal. "Innovation is the life of a business."

The conversation turned to more pleasant topics. Chapal and Marlene finished their coffee and cookies and left to get ready for the evening crowd. Jacob cleaned up and started re-stocking his shelves.

Jacob began laying out his display of three-season gingerbread. He noticed one of the gingerbread men was longer and skinnier than the others. It must have gotten stretched out as he moved it to the pan. Jacob thought the gingerbread man looked a bit like Marlow. The elongated cookie gave him an idea.

A half hour later, Jacob brought a new batch of three season gingerbread men out to the front of the store. This time the tray contained both gingerbread men and gingerbread women. He went to the refrigerator and retrieved some icing he'd made earlier. Jacob decided to finish decorating the batch in the front of the store so he could take care of customers.

The evening customers started arriving not long after he'd finished decorating the first cookie. It was the long and skinny one from the previous batch. As he was ringing up the customer she stared at the cookies in the tray.

"That looks like the spooky guy who owns the furniture store," said the customer.

"Exactly," said Jacob. "I'm going to a meeting with some of the other shopkeepers tonight."

"That's a good idea," said the woman. "Are you going to do one of that funny little man who owns the shoe store?"

"I'm doing one of everyone," said Jacob.

"I'm sure it will be a hit," said the woman as she left the store with her purchases.

Jacob was the first to arrive at the meeting. Marlene was hosting this time. Her home was filled with flowers and assorted bric-a-brac. Jacob found it a bit overwhelming. Once in the living room he set his tray of cookies on the coffee table and took a seat in a large over-stuffed chair. The tray was covered with tin foil. Jacob wasn't going to reveal the cookies until everyone was there.

Carson arrived next, followed by Sofia. Marlow stalked in not long afterward. Chapal soon after. He explained there was problem with one of his suppliers. The Moores were very late. They all chatted about general topics while waiting. Jacob left the cookies covered.

Finally the Moores arrived and Marlene called everyone to attention. Jacob stood up and removed the foil from the top of the cookie tray. Marlene gave each one of them a plate. Jacob followed behind and handed out a specialized cookie to everyone in the group.

Jacob made it a point to start with Marlow's cookie. It was decorated with a suit of dark icing. Carson's cookie had round glasses of thick yellow icing. Chapal's cookie wore a shirt with blue buttons. The cookie's buttons were candy. Sofia's cookie had a gumdrop broche not unlike the one she wore every day.

The Moores' cookies were holding hands. Jacob had made sure the cookies were touching before placing them in the oven. Marlene enjoyed the fact her cookie was significantly rounder than the other ones. The gingerbread men lightened the mood considerably.

"Very amusing" said Marlow. "So what ideas do you have for us young man?"

"I've been talking to Kate," began Jacob. "A lot of fire companies have an annual fair. Most of the time it's in some parking lot off the highway. I was thinking we could block off the streets in town."

"That would require a proposal to the town counsel," said Carson.

"I know," said Jacob. "I spoke to Ted about it. He'll help us talk to the counsel. He thinks they'll go along if the police agree to help."

"How does the fair help us?" asked Sofia.

"Fire company fairs are popular," said Jacob. "Usually a big store or strip mall sponsors them. We could sponsor the fair here and set up special booths to show off our businesses."

"I know lots of people who do crafts and folk art," said Carly. "They could have booths too."

"And local bands," added Howie.

"Nothing too loud," said Marlow.

"We could have games and food and entertainers," said Marlene.

"This is going to take a lot of work," said Carson.

"We'll divide the work up and get help," suggested Chapal. "I believe we can make this happen."

They continued to make plans and delegate the work for several hours. As the meeting broke up Marlene remarked to Jacob it was the longest she could remember. Jacob related the full details of their plans to Kate over dinner the following night.

"I hear the gingerbread men were a hit," said Kate. She was pouring wine for Jacob and herself. Jacob was ladling soup into bowls.

"Everyone seemed to like them," replied Jacob. "It's just the soup and bread for dinner. I hope that's okay."

"I guess you can't expect a baker to cook anything too complex for dinner," said Kate with a smile. "Soup is good."

"My father always made soups for the family when I was growing up," said Jacob. "It was the only thing he made but he was very good at it."

"So cooking does run in your family," said Kate.

"I suppose so," said Jacob. They sat down and started to eat.

"Have you thought about selling the custom gingerbread man?" asked Kate.

"Do you really think people want to buy gingerbread men shaped like Marlow?" replied Jacob.

"Not just tall, scary furniture salesman," said Kate. "I mean like all kinds of jobs. Gingerbread carpenters, doctors, construction workers…"

"We could make one in a business casual," suggested Jacob. "That would cover about half the jobs in America."

Kate laughed. "You get the idea," she said. "Why don't we try making some after dinner?"

"All right," said Jacob.

After they finished eating Jacob cleared the table and they got started. These days he almost always had a batch of three-season gingerbread chilling in the refrigerator. Jacob and Kate decorated the cookies with as many different types of professions they could think up on the spur of the moment.

"This is a good start," said Jacob. "I'll try these out in the shop tomorrow. How do we know we have the right types of jobs, though?"

"Maybe we should ask people," said Kate.

21.

"How many different types of gingerbread do you have now?" asked Carson. He and Chapal had stopped by the bakery for coffee. Jacob had invited them over to discuss the upcoming fair.

"I think over one hundred," said Jacob. "We've only done most of them once, though." He was surprised to learn just how many different jobs existed.

"We?" asked Chapal. "Did you hire an apprentice?"

"Kate has been helping out," said Jacob. "It's easy to make large batches of gingerbread but decorating takes awhile."

"I hope it's not taking her away from organizing the fair," said Carson.

"Don't worry, Carson," said Jacob. "The whole fire department is working on the fair. It's their big event for the year."

"My wife has always helped out at the store," said Chapal. "It is good to have family involved in the business."

Jacob blushed and decided to change the subject. "How are things going with the town council?" he asked.

"Coming along,' said Carson. "They are worried about several things, though."

"They are always worried," said Chapal. "I can talk to them if you want."

"I'm handling it," protested Carson.

"Carson has a lot of experience with the council," said Jacob. "Let's leave things to him."

"Just let us know if you need help," conceded Chapal. "I spoke to the Moores yesterday. Twelve people signed up for craft booths."

"Good," said Jacob. "Marlene has arranged for some local organizations to set up booths as well. Do all the merchants have something to offer in their booth?"

"Everyone except Marlow," said Chapal. "Every time I mention it he mumbles something about not dragging couches out into the street."

They drank their coffee in silence for a few moments. "I'll talk to him," said Jacob finally.

"Do you want me to come along?" asked Chapal.

"No," replied Jacob. "I'll go alone."

The trio finished the rest of their coffee. Carson and Chapal returned to their respective businesses and Jacob cleaned up for the day. He carried the leftover gingerbread men into the kitchen for wrapping.

"They won't keep more than a day or two," said the baker.

"I know," said Jacob. "It's like throwing away little people, though."

"A pie never stares back at you," acknowledged the baker. "You are learning more on your own ever day," said the baker.

"There's still a lot I don't know," replied Jacob.

"You know just about enough to get by," said the baker. "You'll learn the rest over time. You've learned most of what I can teach you."

"I find that hard to believe," objected Jacob.

"The amount of knowledge to be gained through experience is much greater than the amount of knowledge gained through instruction," explained the baker. The baker gestured towards the door to the outer part of the bakery. "You're learning more out there than you do in here."

Jacob nodded and continued wrapping. He finished wrapping and cleaning and had a glass of water. Jacob rinsed out the glass and bid the baker goodnight. He left and locked up the store for the night.

Instead of walking straight home, he turned at the corner and went to the furniture store. At the shop's door he took a deep breath before going inside. Marlow was rubbing at a stain on a couch. Jacob walked over to him.

"The entrance to the apartment is on the side of the building," said Marlow with out looking up. "You should know that by now."

"I was looking for you," replied Jacob.

Marlow didn't answer but continued to clean the stain on the couch. After he'd removed the last crust of it he looked up at Jacob. "Do you need a piece of furniture?" he asked. "I can give you a discount on this couch. As you can see it's been damaged."

"I didn't come to buy furniture," said Jacob.

"You're not here for furniture," continued Marlow, "and you're not here to see the young lady upstairs. What are you here about?"

"I came to talk to you," answered Jacob.

"Very well," said Marlow. "Come into the back. We can talk in my office."

Jacob followed Marlow to the back of the store. He was trying hard to not be scared. It wasn't easy, especially with Marlow leering at him. Marlow led him into a small office and sat down behind a large oak desk.

"What did you want to discuss?" asked Marlow glaring down at him.

"I wanted to see what you were putting in your booth at the fair," said Jacob.

Marlow's initial reply was a deep sigh. "You just walked through the store. What exactly would you suggest I drag out to these silly little tents you and the others intend to erect?"

"Everyone is giving something away as a sample," replied Jacob. "And we're selling other items."

"And what would I give away for free, coffee tables?" asked Marlow sarcastically.

"There must be something," said Jacob. "If we don't bring more people downtown, there won't be customers for you either."

"People always need furniture," said Marlow. "And they always need bread. So I don't see why you care."

"We're trying to help everyone," answered Jacob.

Marlow stared at him for a moment. "You really do care, don't you?" he asked.

"Of course," replied Jacob.

"This isn't the first time business has been slow," said Marlow. "I'm sure it won't be the last. Did you know people used to vacation here?"

"Then everyone lived in the city," continued Marlow. "There were no planes or cruises to exotic places – unless you were rich, of course. Tourists came here to swim and fish in the river. When my grandfather opened the store he sold fancy rocking chairs to tourists."

"I had no idea," said Jacob.

"You should learn more about history," said Marlow. "After my father took over the business the tourists stopped coming and we had to sell more practical furniture. It was like starting all over again."

"Did you work at the store then?" asked Jacob.

"Yes," answered Marlow. "We worked hard to survive. I know you'll find it hard to believe, but I was once ambitious like you."

"So what happened?" asked Jacob.

"As you get older, you see the value in consistency," replied Marlow.

"Slow and steady wins the race?" suggested Jacob.

"There is no race," said Marlow. "That is the point. There are no winners, only survivors."

"That's all I'm trying to do," said Jacob. "Help us all survive."

"I can worry about my own survival," said Marlow. "No offense, Jacob but I've seen men like you before. They have a big plan for bringing new life into these streets. Sooner or later they get bored or distracted."

"When did you get this cynical?" asked Jacob.

"You call it cynical," said Marlow. "I call it realistic."

"Do you have any children, Marlow?" asked Jacob.

"No," replied Marlow. He looked away and Jacob had a feeling he'd hit a nerve.

"Who will take over the furniture store from you?" asked Jacob.

Marlow was quiet for a few moments. "That's not a matter I need to worry about right now," he said finally.

Jacob put his head down. He realized he was already late meeting Kate. "All right," he said. "It's your choice. But it seems to me survival is about taking advantage of your opportunities, not ignoring them."

22.

Jacob was up even earlier than usual on the day of the fair. He hadn't planned to be out quite this early but he was unable to sleep most of the night. The only other person in their booth was Chapal. He was very busy arranging his displays. Jacob nodded to him and started working on his own booth. The others began to arrive soon after.

Marlene was first. She had both of her assistants with her today. Carson and Sofia arrived next. The Moores arrived late as usual. Marlow's booth remained empty. Jacob looked up at the clock tower in the center of town. It was nearly time for the fair to begin and people were already milling around. He looked down the street towards the furniture store. All the lights were off.

"I don't think he's coming," said Chapal. He'd come over to Jacob's booth after finishing with his own. "How did your talk go?"

"As well as you'd expect," replied Jacob.

Chapal nodded. "That one is so stubborn," he said. "What could make a man so hardened and bitter?"

"Loneliness," said Jacob. "When you're alone for long enough you eventually get used to it. Sometimes you forget about other people. If you're lucky, someone reminds you." Jacob glanced over to where Kate was showing some children one of the fire trucks.

"What should we do with his booth?" asked Chapal.

"Let's leave it for now," answered Jacob.

Chapal nodded and returned to his booth. Jacob settled in behind the table he'd erected. He was offering fireman and policeman shaped three-season gingerbread men for free. He was selling several other items including breads, cakes, pies and muffins. He was busy almost immediately as people began purchasing muffins for breakfast.

Jacob found it interesting to watch parents as their children took a gingerbread man. Some parents allowed their children to eat the cookie immediately, despite the hour. For some it was clear the fair was a special occasion. Cookies were certainly not the child's standard breakfast. Other parents seemed to be consistently indulgent; gingerbread for breakfast was not far from the norm.

During spare moments Carson whispered to Jacob that he should be up-selling these parents to the other goods on the table. He noticed Carson made a habit of asking if a customer had socks to go with their new shoes. For dressier shoes he would offer a polishing kit. Once again Jacob realized there was more to Carson than met the eye.

The parents Jacob found most interesting – and yet most uncomfortable – were those who refused to allow their children to unwrap the cookie. "Not for breakfast," they would say, or "after we've had lunch." "You can eat that later if you behave" was another popular refrain. More than half of these parents bought muffins either for themselves or the whole family. Jacob understood his ingredients well enough to know there was a thin line between a muffin and a gingerbread cookie.

Later in the morning Jacob's business slowed down enough for him to relax a bit. It was the awkward couple of hours between breakfast time and lunchtime. Jacob knew from experience patrons would be back in force after they'd eaten their midday meal.

Near the town hall Ted and the other policemen had set up a large grilling area. If things stayed slow he decided he would make his way over for a sandwich.

"Do you have any of those pies with the ivy designs?" said a voice on Jacob's right. He'd been staring at the food in the other direction. He turned to find a smallish, pleasant-looking woman in her seventies or eighties. She was slightly hunched over but still looked spry for her age.

The woman leaned forward as if to tell him a secret. Jacob leaned in as well. "I'm not supposed to have these kinds of things," said the woman, "on account of my blood sugar."

"I have some low sugar and sugar free cookies..." said Jacob.

"Young man," interrupted the woman, "if I want to eat air I'll simply hold my mouth open." Jacob laughed.

"My son and grandson are over by the fire trucks," explained the woman. "They're rather taken with that young woman who's the deputy. This may be my only opportunity."

"Then we'll have to expedite things," said Jacob. "I happen to know that young woman is taken. What is your pleasure?"

"When I was much younger my mother used to take me to the bakery. They always had the most wonderful pies with ivy designs on top," replied the woman. "The baker would always bring out a spoon with the fruit filling on it for me."

Jacob knew the exact pies she was talking about. "I can't do the designs," he replied, "but this pie is made from the same recipe. Would you like a piece?"

"Yes please," replied the woman.

Jacob looked over at Kate's fire truck. He saw two men who looked as though they could be father and son.

They were watching intently as Kate demonstrated some dials on the side of the truck. "I think we have a moment for a slice of pie," said Jacob. He cut two pieces of the baker's spice pie. "On the house," he said as he slipped the woman her piece.

"Thank you very much," replied the woman. She took a bite of her slice. "Just as I remembered it."

"I follow the exact recipe," explained Jacob. "I never tinker around with the baker's signature pies. It's too bad he isn't here. He might remember you."

The woman took another bite of her pie but gave Jacob a confused look. "The baker was an old man when I was a young," said the woman. "You probably know his son."

"I'm pretty sure the baker who taught me started the shop," said Jacob.

As she continued eating her pie the woman described the baker in great detail. Her description matched the baker as Jacob knew him. "That's the baker who taught me," said Jacob.

"The next time you talk to him," said the woman, "find out his secret. If he's the same man, he must be well over a hundred by now."

She finished up the last of her pie and looked over at the fire truck. Jacob followed her gaze. Kate appeared to be excusing herself from the two men. The rest of the crowd was already wandering over to another demonstration.

"Just in time," said the woman. "Thank you again, young man. I feel ten years younger." The woman touched Jacob's arm. "Maybe that's his secret," she said.

"Who's secret?" asked Jacob.

"The baker of course," answered the woman. "Maybe it's the pies that keep him young." She waved goodbye and walked over to the two men at the fire truck.

Jacob was still staring at his own half eaten piece of pie a few moments later when Kate arrived with two plates of food. "No dessert until after you've had lunch," she said. "I'm afraid that rule even applies to bakers."

"I just had an interesting conversation," said Jacob.

"So did I," replied Kate, rolling her eyes.

"I know," said Jacob. "I had pie with their mother."

"Funny, they didn't mention a mother," said Kate. "They were a bundle of cliché's. What was the mother like?"

"She knew the baker," said Jacob, "or at least I think she did."

"What do you mean?" asked Kate taking a bite of her sandwich.

Jacob squeezed in a quick bite of his own before answering. "She knew about his fruit and spice pies," he said.

"With the ivy designs," added Kate.

"Yes," said Jacob. "And she described him perfectly."

"She must know him then," said Kate.

"She also said he was an old man when she was young," said Jacob. "How could he look the same?"

"I don't know," said Kate. "Maybe it was a relative. The baker does seem mysterious. I've never even met him."

"He never comes out to the front of the shop during business hours," replied Jacob.

"He's like the light in the refrigerator," said Kate.

"What?" asked Jacob.

"Didn't you ever try to see if the light in your refrigerator actually goes out when you shut the door?" asked Kate.

"I don't think so," answered Jacob.

"When I was young I used to try shutting the door very slowly to see if the light really went out."

"So you're saying I don't really know if the baker is back there during business hours or not," said Jacob.

"Something like that," said Kate. They ate in silence for a moment. "I guess I'm really saying 'does it matter'?" continued Kate. "He's been your mentor during an important time in your life."

"Yes," confirmed Jacob. "I guess that's enough."

"Sometimes we ruin things if we ask too many questions," said Kate.

"Now that sounds a lot like something the baker once said to me," said Jacob.

"You've always told me he was a wise man," said Kate.

They continued eating until they were distracted by a commotion up the street. The crowd seemed to be shifting in that direction. Jacob and Kate strained to see the source. Jacob dragged a folding chair out from behind the table and stood on it. He looked over the heads of the crowd and instantly recognized the tall form.

Marlow was strolling down the middle of the street pushing a large cart piled high with boxes. As he walked he kept removing long thin objects from the top box and handing one to each person around him.

"What is it?" asked Kate.

"It's Marlow," replied Jacob. "He's giving something out."

"What?" pursued Kate.

"Wait a minute," said Jacob. He continued to watch as Marlow came closer. "He's giving out candlesticks," he concluded.

Marlow pushed the over-loaded cart into his empty booth. He started to set the boxes onto the ground and Jacob walked over to help him. Marlow went back to giving out the candlesticks as Jacob organized the boxes. Jacob took a closer look at one of the sticks. It looked as though Marlow had carved them by hand.

Kate came over to the booth. Marlow reached over and handed her two candlesticks. "One for you and one for my assistant here," said Marlow gesturing at Jacob.

"These are handsome," said Jacob. "Did you carve them?"

"These days I use power tools," replied Marlow. "But my brother and I used to carve them. Would you like to hear the story?"

"Yes, please," replied Kate. Several people in the crowd also encouraged him to continue. Everyone seemed fascinated and Jacob understood every child in town must have found Marlow just as intimidating.

"I started making these when I was child," explained Marlow. "My father used to travel on business. Sometimes we wouldn't see him for several weeks. During those times my brothers and I would spend the time carving candlesticks like these. When they were finished we'd place them in the windows with a lit candle. We kept them burning until my father came home."

Marlow held up one of the candlesticks and lifted himself up in stature. He appeared to grow even taller in that instant. "My mother used to tell us the candlesticks would help my father find his way home. May these candlesticks always help your wandering relatives find their way home."

Jacob looked up at Marlow and for the first time he felt no fear. Marlow made a slight movement with his head that Jacob interpreted as a nod. He smiled at

Marlow. Kate stood on her toes to give him a quick peck on the cheek. Jacob tried to think of something to say but decided it was Marlow who should have the last word.

23.

Four days after the fair Jacob and Kate were still working on custom cookie orders. Jacob could smell gingerbread dough on his hands and happily thought it might be weeks before the scent faded from his skin.

"I think we have one more afternoon's work," said Kate as they were cleaning up. "Then we should be all caught up." She handed Jacob the order list.

"Maybe less," replied Jacob. "We seem to be getting faster."

"I agree," said Kate. She washed her hands in the sink. "I'd better get going. We have a meeting with the auxiliary tonight."

"Thanks again for your help," said Jacob.

"You know you're welcome," answered Kate. She gave him a gingerbread-flavored kiss and left for the evening.

Not long after she'd gone Jacob heard a knock from the front of the shop. He quickly wiped his hands on a nearby towel and walked out of the kitchen. Ted was standing outside the glass door. Jacob waved and hurried over to let him into the bakery.

"Hello, Ted," said Jacob. "What can I get you?"

"Nothing for me, thanks," replied Ted. He seemed to reconsider and asked Jacob if he had any coffee.

"I think there's still some left over," said Jacob. "But it's been in the pot awhile."

"That'll be fine," said Ted. "Let's talk in the kitchen."

"Sure," said Jacob.

"I wanted to wait until Kate left," said Ted once they reached the kitchen.

Jacob looked over at Ted. For the first time since he'd met him, Ted wore a somber expression. "What's wrong, Ted?" asked Jacob.

"I think we have a problem," replied Ted.

By the time Ted finished explaining the situation, Jacob had drank most of the stale coffee himself. Ted barely touched his first cup. Jacob didn't recognize a lot of the legal words but understood enough to realize what Ted was telling him. It was the worst that could happen.

"You have a lot of friends in town," said Ted. "We'll help until we can get it all sorted out. It's not unusual for small business owners to skip a few steps." Ted glanced down at the series of papers he'd brought with him. "Of course, you seem to have skipped all the steps."

"Believe me, Ted," said Jacob, "I thought I was working for the baker."

"If the baker is as wise as you say," replied Ted. "He should have known about the paperwork involved. You can't just pick a vacant store and open a business - especially not a business where you serve food."

"I just can't believe there aren't any permits," said Jacob, "or any type of ownership."

Ted looked through the stack of papers. "According to this," explained Ted, "the building is in some type of probate. You'll have to close for a while but we're going to help you fix this.

"Probate?" asked Jacob. "I don't believe this is happening."

"If we can solve the ownership problem the town is prepared to fast track your permits," continued Ted. "We even called in some favors with the county."

"What if we can't sort out the problem with the building?" asked Jacob.

"I don't know what your financial situation is but the other merchants are committed to helping you rent or buy another building in town."

"I feel like this bakery is my home," said Jacob, "and the baker's home."

"Where is the baker?" asked Ted.

"I don't know," said Jacob. "He actually hasn't been in since before the fair. I just thought he was letting me handle things on my own."

"He's certainly letting you handle things now," replied Ted. Ted stood up and put a hand on Jacob's shoulder. "Take some time to think. You can't open tomorrow so use the time to talk to the baker. I'll come by after my shift and go over the next steps with you."

After Ted left, Jacob stared down at the papers without actually looking at them. He had worked hard over the last few months. Now he might have to start all over again. What must Marlene and the others think of him? He felt like he had been masquerading. Jacob had no idea what he would tell Kate.

Jacob sat for a few more minutes and then went back to cleaning. As he started putting items away, however he found himself rummaging through the cabinets. Eventually Jacob began to take items out of the various cabinets and closets. He was looking for something – anything about the baker or the shop itself.

All he could find were items related to baking. There was nothing about the baker or the shop itself. "Everything here is perishable," he said out loud. Jacob emptied the cabinets and pantry. The countertops were filled with items stacked on top of items. He failed to find any information about the bakery or the baker.

Then Jacob had a thought. He left the kitchen and looked at the glass display case. He could see there was nothing in there to provide a clue. Then Jacob noticed a wood panel underneath the display. The first few inches of the display were enclosed in wood to support the display and conceal the refrigeration unit.

Jacob unlatched and removed the rear panel revealing the cooling mechanism underneath. As he pulled back the panel he saw an object flutter to the ground. He rooted around behind the display case. The object turned out to be an old black and white photograph. The photo had picked up a yellowish tint and one corner was torn off.

Jacob instantly recognized the figure in the photograph. It was the baker. Jacob looked at the picture closely. He could tell the photo had been taken in front of the display case but couldn't be sure it was in this building. In his hands the baker was holding an ivy-decorated pie. Even in the small photo Jacob could see the intricacy of the ivy design.

In the picture the baker smiled with pride. Jacob turned the photograph over but it was blank. He looked back in the area under the display but there was nothing else. Jacob replaced the panel and took the photograph back into the kitchen.

Jacob set the photograph on the table and looked at the mess in the kitchen. He decided he could not leave the bakery in its currently disheveled condition. Jacob returned all the items to the appointed places within the cabinets and pantry. He swept up the floor and wiped down the countertops as he would any other night.

When he was finished Jacob took a step back to check over the kitchen, just as he did every night before he left. Everything appeared to be in its place. The photograph sat on the table where he'd left it. Jacob picked it up and put it in his pocket. He took another long look around the kitchen and walked back out to the front of the store.

Jacob examined the shelves, counters and display. Everything seemed in order except for a small smudge he'd left on the display counter earlier. Jacob walked up the display and used his shirt to gently rub off the smudge. Jacob walked slowly and deliberately to the front door. He took a deep breath and opened the door. The air seemed colder than it should have been.

24.

The old question was back in Jacob's mind again as he unlocked the bakery the next morning. What's the worst that could happen? He would have to close the bakery. He would have to fill out a lot of paperwork. He might have to pay a fine. He would have to start over in another building here in town. He might have to rely on other people for help.

The prospects didn't seem so bad after all. He had grown fond of the building, but he could grow to love another. As long as he had an oven, good ingredients and customers everything would be fine. Jacob remembered he also had Kate.

Ted had advised Jacob to remove any personal items in the shop for now. Jacob half-heartedly started filling a cardboard box with some of his own cooking utensils. Jacob gave up on the box and decided to start with the refrigerator.

He had one batch of still undecorated three-season gingerbread cookies. There was also an extra batch of dough and a few containers of fruit. Jacob took the tray of gingerbread men out of the refrigerator and set them on the counter. He thought he might take them home. Jacob was preparing to wrap the unbaked cookies when he heard a knock at the door. At first Jacob wasn't going to answer. He arrived later than usual but had left the closed sign on the door. The oven wasn't pre-heated so there was no scent of fresh baked bread or cake.

Then Jacob thought it might be Ted or Kate so he left the kitchen and went to the front door. On the other side of the door was a man Jacob didn't know. The man wore the blackest suit and deepest frown Jacob had ever seen. Jacob was sure the man was with the board of health or a similar body. Still he tried to make his way to the front door with a smile.

"I'm sorry but we're closed for today," said Jacob.

"I have a matter of business to discuss with you," said the man. "I'm an attorney with the law firm of Arcadio and Aureliano. I represent the owner of this property."

"Come in," said Jacob. He started to say more but the man in the dark suit held up his hand.

"Allow me to explain my presence," said the attorney. "I am here on behalf of the owner to sell you this shop. If you are interested in the property, that is."

"Definitely," said Jacob. "But I don't have a lot of money."

"Just a moment," said the attorney. He took a pair of spectacles out of his breast pocket and rested them on the bridge of his nose. Next he took some papers out of a large black leather bag. The attorney in the dark suit read through the papers. "This transaction does not involve standard currency," said the man.

"I don't think I understand," said Jacob.

"This property is for sale to you, and you only, for the sum of one pie," replied the attorney.

Jacob started to answer but again the attorney held up his hand. "Allow me to finish please," he requested. "The pie must be made here in this shop, using only ingredients and tools available in this kitchen. It must be baked using the oven on these premises. The recipe for the pie should be identical to the first pie you made in these ovens. The pie must be decorated with such flourishes as to express the baker's skill and artistry."

The man was silent for several minutes. "Well?" asked the man finally.

"Yes?" answered Jacob tentatively.

"I suggest you get started," said the attorney.

Jacob led the man into the kitchen and offered him a stool at the worktable in the center. The attorney sat down and took out a newspaper with writing Jacob did not recognize. He glanced at Jacob one more time and then buried his head behind the paper. Jacob started the oven.

Jacob retrieved the necessary spices from the cabinets. He had enough of the correct fruit but decided to cut fresh pieces. Jacob heard nothing more from the man in the dark suit except for the occasional ruffling of his newspaper.

Jacob knew baking the fruit and spice pie would not pose a problem for him. The designs on top would be a problem. It had been easy for the baker to teach him the ingredients and steps to make the fruit and spice pie. But Jacob had never been able to duplicate the delicate slices needed to produce the ivy shapes from the dough.

"The pie must be decorated with such flourishes as to express the baker's skill and artistry." That is what the attorney said. Jacob turned to the man in the dark suit. "Can I try multiple pies?" asked Jacob.

The man in the dark suit put his paper down and stared at Jacob. He looked through the documents he had brought with him. "You may bake as many pies as you like," said the man finally, "but you may choose only one to present to me."

Jacob nodded and went back to work. It made sense. He could try multiple times and then pick the best attempt. Jacob made enough of the low protein dough mixture to make several pies. During the first rise he cut up the fruit and prepped seven pans for baking. Jacob checked the temperature of the oven several times.

There was still time to wait after Jacob had mixed the fruit and spice into a large batch of filling. He decided to try engaging the attorney in conversation. Perhaps he could learn more about the baker. "How long have you known the baker?" asked Jacob.

The attorney did not react, except an occasional turn of his newspaper. "How long have you known the baker?" asked Jacob again. There was another pause and another change of page. Jacob decided to try a more general question. "Is your firm located nearby?"

The attorney put down his paper and stared at Jacob again. "I assume this delay is necessary to the process?" he asked.

"Yes," replied Jacob. "The dough must rise. I've already done the other steps."

The man nodded his head once in understanding. "Would you like a section of the newspaper to read?" he asked.

"No thank you," said Jacob. "I have some other work I can do." The man in the dark suit resumed reading his newspaper.

Jacob removed some leftover dough from the refrigerator and rolled it out. While the dough continued to rise he practiced cutting the ivy flourishes. By the time the dough was ready to be beaten down his designs had improved. However the flourishes were still not very impressive - certainly not enough to buy the shop, decided Jacob.

Jacob beat down the dough and continued practicing as he waited for the second rise. Near the end of the second rise Jacob realized he had reached a point where his skill with the knife simply wasn't getting any better. He let out a large sigh and looked over to see if the attorney had noticed. The man continued to read his newspaper.

Finally Jacob began to roll out the dough. Jacob cut out the bottom sections of the crust and laid one in each pan. Next he cut out the top portion of each crust. He poured the right amount of filling in each pie and set the top pieces of dough in place. Jacob trimmed the edges and cut small slits on the tops of the pies so they could vent while cooking.

Jacob could not put off the decoration any longer so he began to cut the ivy shapes. It was difficult to equal the baker's skill. Jacob decorated the pies one at a time with the ivy designs. Occasionally he would glance at the photograph of the baker he'd found the day before. His flourishes were poor substitutes for the baker's fine latticework.

Jacob stopped before decorating the seventh pie. Listening to his heart, he placed one of the unbaked gingerbread men on the center of the pie. In the first light-hearted moment he'd had in several hours Jacob took out his gingerbread decorations and finished off the cookie on top of the pie. This gingerbread man was a little baker.

Jacob put all the pies in the oven and sat down at the center table opposite the attorney in the dark suit. The man did not look up. Jacob stared at the newspaper pages in front of him. All of the words were foreign to him so he passed the time making up ideas about what the articles might be about.

The smell of baking pies gradually filled the kitchen and the man in the dark suit put down his newspaper. Without a word he folded up the paper and placed it in a separate pocket in the document bag he'd brought with him. Jacob got up and took two plates out of one of the cabinets. He also set out two coffee cups. From a drawer he got two forks and placed them next to the plates.

Jacob poked his head into the oven before starting the coffee. The pies were coming out nicely - just the right shade of brown. The ivy designs and the gingerbread man had fused themselves to the tops of their respective pies. Jacob took out the pies and set them on the counter to cool while the coffee brewed.

Jacob examined each of the ivy pies to determine the best one. The second and third seemed slightly better than the rest so he slid those forward. As the last drips of coffee fell into the waiting pot Jacob tried to decide between the two remaining pies. He decided to pour the coffee first as a stall.

"Thank you," said the attorney.

"Cream and sugar?" asked Jacob.

"Black is fine," replied the man. Jacob did not really find this surprising. He poured a cup of coffee for himself and returned the pot to the warmer.

Jacob went back to the pies. Out of the two he'd slid forward, the one on the left appeared slightly better. He picked up the pie and turned to face the attorney. The man looked at him expectantly but Jacob hesitated. He turned back to the counter and put the pie back.

"The pie must be decorated with such flourishes as to express the baker's skill and artistry," Jacob recalled again. He looked at the flour beneath his fingernails. He realized he was the baker now. He was the gingerbread man. Jacob grabbed the seventh pie - the one decorated with the baker gingerbread man and lifted it off the counter.

Jacob served the man in the dark suit a piece from the seventh pie. The man took one bite of his slice of pie. He chewed carefully and washed it down with a sip of coffee. He looked up at Jacob. "Please wrap this piece and the rest of the pie," said the attorney.

As Jacob wrapped the pie the attorney withdrew several documents from his bag. He spread them out on the table and made several circles in pen. After Jacob had wrapped the pie the man handed him the pen. "Sign next to every circle," instructed the attorney.

Jacob did as he was told. After he was finished the attorney gathered up the papers. He tore pink copies off several of them and handed them to Jacob. The rest he placed back into his bag. "Our business is concluded," said the attorney. He took the rest of his pie and left the shop.

25.

"That is amazing," said Kate as Jacob finished telling her the story of the man in the dark suit for the second time. "Tell me again."

Before Jacob could start again there was a knock at his door. He went out into the living room and looked out the window. Ted stood on the porch. Jacob opened the door and Ted entered. He had a handful of papers with him.

"These arrived by messenger a little awhile ago," said Ted. "The probate was settled. You own the bakery. Tomorrow we're going to fast track your other paperwork. I think we can have you back open in a day or two."

"That's great news," said Kate coming into the living room.

"How did you settle with the owner?" asked Ted. "How did you even find the owner?"

"The owner found me," replied Jacob. "An attorney came to see me today. He sold me the bakery for a pie."

'For a pie?" asked Ted.

"For a pie," repeated Kate. "Can you believe it?"

"I have to believe it," answered Ted. "All the proper paperwork says so."

Two days later Jacob was back at the bakery finishing up the orders he had taken during the fair. Several customers remarked they were glad to see the shop open again and Jacob had a new appreciation for every item and each transaction.

He savored every moment of the slowdown between the morning and evening rush. Making the custom gingerbread was still Jacob's favorite part of the business. The little men became his trademark and he used them on pies, cakes and other goods.

Decorating pies always made him think of the baker and he wondered if he'd ever see his mentor again. The ceremony with the attorney seemed final but he could not imagine the baker not offering any final words of wisdom or at least saying "goodbye." Still, Jacob recognized the finality in his recent conversations with the baker. "I have taught you all I can...the rest you must learn out there," he recalled the old man's words.

Jacob's increased appreciation for his business gave him an idea. After work he walked over to the flower stop to speak with Marlene. He took some cupcakes. Jacob did not want to arrive at the flower shop empty-handed.

"Hello Jacob," said Marlene. She was behind the counter putting the finishing touches on several matching arrangements. "Wedding center pieces," she explained.

"They look nice," replied Jacob. "I brought you some cupcakes."

"Thank you," said Marlene. "Congratulations on buying the bakery. I always assumed it was your shop."

"I know," said Jacob. "I'm glad things are settled. I'm really happy to be back at work."

"I understand what you mean completely," said Marlene.

"I think we can give more people a chance to have that feeling," said Jacob. "Remember all those people who had booths at the fair?"

"Most of those people couldn't afford to buy or even rent a storefront," said Marlene.

"I know," said Jacob. "But we have several vacant stores in town. Why can't we let people use that space on the weekends?"

"If Carson were here I'm sure he'd warn us about the town counsel," said Marlene. "It's an intriguing idea, though."

"Might bring more people downtown," suggested Jacob.

"True," said Marlene. "Do you have a plan?"

"I thought I'd see what you thought first," answered Jacob. "I should talk to Carson next."

"Good idea," said Marlene. "This is one of the evenings he stays late for inventory. He should still be there."

"Thanks, Marlene," said Jacob.

"Since you're going over," said Marlene, "you should share some of these cupcakes with him."

"Excellent idea," agreed Jacob. He took half the cup cakes off the plate and walked to the shoe store. The front light was out and the closed sign was on the door but Jacob could see a light coming from a back room. He knocked on the front door and waved at Carson. After realizing it was Jacob, Carson came over to the door and unlocked it.

"Good evening," said Carson as he opened the door.

"Hello Carson," said Jacob. "I brought you some cupcakes...and I wanted to talk to you about an idea."

"Come in," said Carson. "I could use a break."

Once inside Jacob explained the idea. At first Carson seemed skeptical but after considering it and munching on a cupcake he was slightly more positive. "The town would require the craft merchants to pay some sort of use tax, of course," said Carson.

'That's fair," said Jacob. "Could we base that on actual sales?"

"I suppose," said Carson. "Most of the storefronts are owned by private individuals, though. They would have to agree to the plan and they might want a share of the sales."

"Are they making anything on the buildings now?" asked Jacob.

"I suppose not," said Carson.

"Even a small percentage of the profits is more than they are making now," said Jacob.

"It is logical," agreed Carson. "It will take awhile to arrange." Carson was quiet for a time. "I'll look into it," he said finally. "I'll talk to the town council and the building owners."

"Thank you Carson," said Jacob.

"Thank you, Jacob," replied Carson.

26.

Jacob was preparing for the day's baking when he paused to stare at the picture of the baker. "That was taken a long time ago," said a voice from behind him.

Jacob turned around to find the baker standing there. It was the first time Jacob had seen him since he'd purchased the bakery for a pie. "Hello," said Jacob.

"You are doing well," said the baker.

"I still have a lot to learn," said Jacob.

"Yes you do," said the baker. "But the rest you can learn on your own."

"You sound as though you are leaving," said Jacob.

The baker was silent. He busied himself examining some rolls Jacob had recently removed from the oven. "These are better than last week's batch."

"About the shop..." began Jacob.

The baker held up his hand. "There's no need to speak of such things. You keep what you earn," he said.

The baker returned to the rolls. "These are better than last week's batch. Next week's batch will be better than these." He looked over at Jacob and smiled.

"How can you be sure I'll keep getting better?" asked Jacob.

"Because," replied the baker with a twinkle in his eye, 'I kept getting better." The baker untied this apron and took it off. He folded the apron several times and tucked it under his arm.

"Always keep getting better," said the baker. "Stay on your feet and they'll never catch you." The baker began to move towards the door. "And beware the fox."

That night Jacob dreamed about the baker and his pies. The baker was making his ivy designs. A woman and a little girl were in the shop. Jacob was sure the little girl was the old woman he'd met at the fair.

"Beware the fox," whispered Jacob as he sat up in bed. A moment later his alarm went off.

The words stayed with Jacob as he went about his morning routine and throughout the early rush. After the morning customers had left Jacob did something he had not done since his first day working at the shop. He closed the bakery for lunch. Instead of eating in the kitchen he left the shop and went to the library.

The library was a small brick building at the edge of the business district. In truth it wasn't a library in the way most people thought of one. None of the books were meant to be checked out – not that anyone would want to check one out. The town library held only books and records about the town itself.

Jacob stepped into the building for the first time in his life. He must have appeared lost because the librarian called out to him from the other side of the room. "Can I help you, sir?" he asked.

"I'm looking for information about one of the shops in town," answered Jacob.

The librarian came over to a counter at the front of the library. "We have information about most of the structures," he replied. "I personally know many of the histories. You'd like to know about the bakery."

"Yes," said Jacob. Surely this must be fate. "How did you know?"

"Simple," said the librarian. "You're the baker." The librarian picked up a cookie from underneath the counter and took a bite. It was half eaten but Jacob could still recognize it as one of his own.

"What can you tell me?" asked Jacob.

"The building you occupy was built in 1924," began the librarian, "same year as most of the structures on that block."

"Who built the bakery?" probed Jacob.

"A land speculator," said the librarian. "He sold the bakery and the other stores to the original merchants."

"Who bought the bakery?" continued Jacob.

"That," replied the librarian, "I would have to look up." The librarian went to a large filing cabinet on the left side of the room. He opened a drawer and ran his fingers over a number of files. The librarian pulled a file from the back of the drawer and brought it over to the counter.

"This file has the land purchases from the year the building was constructed," said the librarian. "The name we're looking for should be in here. The librarian leafed through the pages several times. His expression increasingly became a frown.

"This is odd," concluded the librarian. "I don't have any of the sales records for that building."

"There was a fire at the courthouse that year," said a familiar voice from the back. It was Marlow. He came out from behind a dark bookcase. Marlow was carrying a large binder with old newspapers.

"I don't remember a fire," said the librarian.

"You only remember the good events," replied Marlow.

"You only remember the bad ones," countered the librarian.

"That's probably true," agreed Jacob. "How long have you been here?" he asked Marlow.

"I'm here every day from noon until two," answered Marlow. "I come to read the old newspapers."

"Were you going to say hello?" asked Jacob. He knew it was a silly question as soon as he asked. Of course Marlow wouldn't greet him. It was nothing personal. It was just Marlow.

Jacob turned back to the librarian. "Is there any way to find out who owned the building?" he asked.

"What about the ownership paperwork you signed the other day?" suggested Marlow. "That would have the seller's name."

"The bakery was in some sort of probate," replied Jacob. "The papers are in the name of the attorneys on behalf of the seller's estate."

"So we have a mystery," said the librarian. "I enjoy mysteries."

Marlow shook his head and checked his watch. "I've wasted enough of my lunch break on this nonsense," he said. He took his binder of newspapers and returned to his place behind the dark bookcase.

"Sometimes I wish Marlow didn't come to visit every day," said the librarian.

"I can still hear you," called Marlow from the back.

The librarian rolled his eyes. "I can do some research with the county," he said. "I believe I have some photos of your building as well. I'll have to locate them in the archives."

Jacob had the feeling the "archives" meant another row of file cabinets or possibly a back room. "I'd appreciate that," he said.

"Come back next week," said the librarian. "I should have something by then."

Jacob thought about suggesting the librarian just call when he had located additional information. However, he understood the librarian was looking for a reason for him to visit again. Even if their exchange consisted of "nothing yet...maybe next week" it would still represent human contact for the librarian.

Jacob shook the librarian's hand and called "goodbye" to Marlow. He heard a grunt from the back in response. Jacob chuckled and returned to the bakery to prepare for the evening rush.

27.

Jacob looked down at his latest batch of custom gingerbread men. They looked like a small cookie army of tradespeople. Jacob picked up a clipboard with the orders. He checked the list against each cookie on the tray to make sure he hadn't missed any. He had one last cookie to decorate. Jacob iced the cookie in a blue skirt and jacket with a small piece of licorice and gumdrop as a microphone. He decided it was a reasonable enough representation of a reporter and checked it off the list.

When a reporter arrived later to pick up the cookie she announced she wanted to interview Jacob. She had heard about the three-season gingerbread and custom cookies. She called it a "human interest story." During the interview he decorated a fresh gingerbread man to look like the cameraman who came with her.

The reporter seemed rather rushed and mentioned several times she and the camera man had three more stops after the bakery. Jacob tried to interest her in the efforts to bring more shoppers downtown. She only seemed interested in the gingerbread men.

After several predictable questions the reporter thanked Jacob and the cameraman packed up his gear. Jacob gave the reporter and the cameraman an assortment of other goods from the shop. After they left he cleaned and closed the bakery as usual. Jacob headed home to dinner with Kate.

After dinner Jacob and Kate had a visit from Carson, who had become increasingly more social. He even agreed to stay and have dessert with them. Of course, Jacob's carrot cake was considered hard to resist by most people who had tried it. Carson announced he had been successful with the town council. It seemed his years of proper procedure and letter writing had paid off. The council trusted his judgment enough to agree to the weekend craft booths.

Three of the owners of the vacant storefronts had agreed to participate in the weekend craft booths – provided the town carried the responsibility of clean up and maintenance. They also wanted a percentage of the profits. Jacob thought that was reasonable and suggested they use another slice of the profits to cover these costs.

Carson triumphantly informed them he had already gotten the council to agree to provide the budget for at least the first few weeks. Carson thought they might be able to get started soon and Jacob suggested they start advertising.

As they were finishing up their cake and conversation there was a knock at the door. Jacob opened the door to find Marlene. She rushed in and ran straight to the television in the living room. Kate and Carson came out in the meantime. Marlene turned on the set and quickly flipped to a specific channel.

"Wait, wait," said Marlene. "They're supposed to re-run it at seven."

"Re-run what?" asked Kate.

"The story," said Marlene. "Jacob's story."

A few minutes later the story came on the television. All the footage had been spliced together in a way Jacob didn't remember but it seemed to work in its own way.

As Jacob decorated the gingerbread man the reporter spoke about how Jacob had opened the bakery several months ago and created three-season gingerbread and the custom gingerbread men. The story ended with a suggestion that all her viewers visit the bakery to check out his unique cast of characters and hint of the holiday season.

"This is really big, isn't it?" asked Carson.

"Let's not get ahead of ourselves," said Jacob. "This is definitely a bit of good luck. But we shouldn't set expectations too high." He had experienced this type of promise in his life before: the hint of a possible promotion, a friend of friend with a break through product, an uncle with an idea for a business they could start together.

"Jacob's right," said Kate. "Let's wait and see how things play out but I'm sure it will be good."

"But I don't think 'big' is the right word, Carson," said Jacob.

"Somewhat famous" were the words Kate had used after the rush the next day. Jacob decided he liked that description. Through a few twists of fate, the reporter's story about Jacob was picked up by the national news as part of a larger story on small town business.

Morning in the bakery went as usual. Commuters came in on their way to the train. They purchased bagels, rolls and muffins for breakfast. However, almost all of them placed an order for one or more of the custom gingerbread men. One man wanted an order for his entire office. For the first time Jacob had to tell a customer an order would take more than a day or two to complete.

The afternoon brought the real rush, though. Jacob served all of his usual customers along with many new people who came in specifically because of the news story. Jacob had to ask Kate for help filling the orders. She brought dinner to the shop and they worked late into the night baking gingerbread and decorating the cookies.

After catching up the first day Jacob learned to use the slower time in the late morning and early afternoon to bake and decorate extra gingerbread men. He also began to create several types of basic figures he could turn into more customized gingerbread men.

Jacob started making deposits in his bank account for the first time in many months. He finally had the confidence to do something he'd put off since the day he'd walked out of his office. Jacob called his parents.

"Hello Jacob," said his mother. "It's good to hear from you. How are you?"

"I'm fine," replied Jacob. "Is everything okay with you and dad?"

"Yes," said his mother. "Jacob, how are things at work?"

"Work is good," said Jacob. He'd said that to his mother before, but this time he meant it. "That's one of the reasons I called."

"Because your father thought he saw you in a news story," continued his mother, "something about you working in a bakery."

"I'm a baker now," explained Jacob. "I left my old job because I wasn't really happy."

"So the story was true," said his mother. Jacob heard her say something to his father in the background. In the distance his father replied. "He said the story made you look very successful."

"It's going well, mom," said Jacob. "I met a baker who helped me learn the trade. Every day I make bread, muffins, cookies and cakes."

"You always did like to make cookies," answered his mother. Jacob heard his mother talking to his father again. "Your father said the reporter mentioned something about gingerbread men."

"Gingerbread is my signature product at the bakery," explained Jacob. "I decorate them for different jobs. They've become very popular."

"That sounds nice," said his mother. "Did you know you wanted to bake when you quit your other job?"

Jacob hesitated. He wasn't sure how his parents would take the news that he just left his old job with no prospects. "No," he said finally. "To be honest I just stopped doing my old job. I wasn't sure what I wanted to be."

"Sometimes you need to take some time and figure things out," said his mother. "Just don't forget to make sure you have some stability."

"So you and dad aren't disappointed?" asked Jacob.

"To be honest, dear," said his mother, "we never really understood what you did before anyway."

"Neither did I," replied Jacob.

28.

Jacob pulled the truck into the fruit distributor and parked. Two nearby workers recognized the pickup and began placing his usual order in the bed. Jacob got out and jumped into the truck bed to help them slide the crates. His supply runs were now down to only two stops. The flour merchant delivered to the bakery each day. Likewise the dairy brought fresh milk, cream and eggs each day.

Jacob also got a daily delivery of staple fruits such as apples, pears and bananas. However, he still visited the warehouse at least once a week to see what was in season or unusual. He also enjoyed talking with the owner, Freda. She came over as the workers finished loading the truck and Jacob jumped down.

"Anything interesting today?" asked Jacob.

"I have fresh mulberries today," replied the Freda.

"I haven't baked with them yet," said Jacob. "What do they taste like?"

"See for yourself," replied Freda. She led Jacob over to a table with several crates of a black fruit in tight bunches. Freda plucked a cluster off the bunch, wiped it on her apron and handed it to Jacob.

Jacob took a bite of the fruit and swished the juice around in his mouth. He found the mulberry to be a bold taste containing both sweet and tart. "Very interesting," said Jacob.

"Mulberries always remind me of the taste of grapefruit, but with a twist," said Freda.

"Yes," agreed Jacob. "It definitely has its own distinct taste. I would describe it as assertive and confident. It has strength and balance." The fruit reminded him of Kate.

"Your palette has really improved," said Freda. "And I like the words you pick. You always talk about the fruit as if it has a personality."

"I think it does," said Jacob. He took another bite of the mulberries. "I wonder how these would taste in a muffin. I could add some sour cream and apple sauce."

"Try adding some almonds as well," suggested the fruit merchant.

"I'll do that," said Jacob.

"You know, the mulberries are a multiple fruit," said Freda.

"I remember," said Jacob, recalling their conversation of several weeks ago.

"How do you feel about multiples now?" asked Freda.

"There may be hope," replied Jacob. "There are some fruits that are happy enough to go along for the ride but others are more challenging. Both have their merits."

"Well put," said Freda. "How is business?"

"Good," said Jacob. "I really enjoy the work."

"I remember a time when you would have answered that question based on revenue," observed Freda. "How is Kate?"

"She's like the mulberries," said Jacob.

Freda laughed. "I'd better let you get back on your way," she said. "I know you probably have to stop at the spice merchant."

"Yes," confirmed Jacob. "He won't deliver to me."

"The spice merchant doesn't deliver to anyone," said Freda. "I think he's just likes to talk to people."

"I think he just likes to talk near people," said Jacob.

"Well put," said Freda.

"I'll bring you some of the first batch of mulberry muffins," said Jacob. He picked up a crate of mulberries and carried it to the truck. The bed was already loaded with his usual order so he placed the crate in the passenger side seat. Jacob waved to Freda and started on his way.

Jacob left the fruit distributor and continued on to the spice merchant. He was engaged with another customer when Jacob arrived. Jacob glanced at the shelves while he waited. He also stayed close enough to listen in on the merchant's conversation with the customer.

"For that I recommend kaffir lime," said the spice merchant. "I have some here."

"I've never worked with that," replied the customer. "Can't I just use some lemon-lime extract?"

"It wouldn't be the same," replied the spice merchant. Jacob watched from the corner of his eye. "You're making a Thai dish. Kaffir lime provides distinct flavor to those dishes," continued the spice merchant.

"I really don't want to mess it up," said the customer. She put the container of kaffir lime down. "Do you have any lime extract?"

"Try the supermarket," replied the spice merchant with a scow. The customer left in a huff and he dismissed her with a wave of his hand. "Who's next," he announced.

"I'm the only other person here," said Jacob.

"Then you're next," answered the spice merchant. "Let's see your list for today." Jacob handed over the list.

The spice merchant began to fill a box with various spices and herbs. "With the old one it was that concoction of spices for his pies," mumbled the spice merchant as he worked. "With this young one it's ginger, always with the ginger."

"I'm making gingerbread men," clarified Jacob.

"Gingerbread men?" asked the spice merchant. "This time of year?"

"I sell them all year round now," confirmed Jacob.

"And people buy them?" asked the spice merchant.

"Yes," said Jacob. "I modified the recipe. It's called three-season gingerbread. People like it all year - it reminds them of the holidays."

The spice merchant chuckled to himself as he filled the box with containers of ginger and molasses. "Gingerbread out of season," he said.

"I'm surprised," said Jacob. "I thought you of all people would favor experimentation."

"You misunderstand my laughter," replied the spice merchant. "I do not seek to mock your invention."

The spice merchant leaned forward and gestured for Jacob to do the same. "I'll let you in on a secret," he said. "Some people think this is a spice and herb shop. But it's actually a magic shop." The spice merchant gave Jacob a wink. "Think about the simplest thing you bake: a loaf of bread," he said.

"I think I know what you mean," replied Jacob. For him the spice merchant, the fruit vender and the dairy were all magic shops. For a painter the art store was a magic shop. For a carpenter the hardware store was a magic shop.

The firehouse was Kate's magic shop. Fire was like the bread. Flame lived and breathed oxygen. It rose and fell. With the proper tools, Kate could control it. That was magic too. Jacob realized they were all magicians in one way or another – and that meant anyone could become one. You simply had to create something, make something or be something.

"And always be true to yourself." The words had come from Jacob's mind but he knew they belonged to the baker. "That is the final principle, the most important. Remember that one and you are unlikely to forget the others."

Jacob reached into his back pocket and pulled out a ragged slip of paper. On it he'd written all the principles the baker had taught him:

Always look for the logical order of things.
Always batch similar tasks.
Always start early and work on the hardest parts first.
Always use the right tool for the right job.
Always make sure you are ready for ingredients to mix.
Always take the time to learn a skill right.
Always concentrate on the task at hand as if it is the most important.
Always know what you want to create before you start.
Always taste your own work.
Always present your creations honestly but with flair.
Always give up that which you have in excess.
Always sell only items worthy of your craft.
Always make things the appropriate size.
Always find something unique you can offer people.
Always keep getting better.

Jacob pulled a pen from his shirt pocket and added the last principle:

"Always be true to yourself."

Jacob carefully folded the paper and put it back in his pocket before returning to the bakery.

29.

The following week Jacob returned to the library. His success at the bakery had only increased his curiosity about the baker. He also felt somewhat obligated to visit the librarian again. He couldn't imagine spending all day alone in a building, with only Marlow as a visitor. Predictably, the librarian was happy to see Jacob when he arrived.

"Ah, the baker," said the librarian. "A lot has happened since the last time you were here."

"You've heard about the news story?" asked Jacob.

"I read more than just these old books," said the librarian gesturing around the room.

"Of course," said Jacob. "Have you found anything about the baker or the building?"

"I wasn't able to find anything more about the buyer of the building," replied the librarian, "but I did locate some pictures you might find interesting."

The librarian ducked underneath the counter and returned with a manila folder. He set the folder down on the counter and opened it. Inside was a stack of pictures. Jacob instantly recognized the picture on top – it was the same one he'd found at the bakery. "That's the baker," said Jacob.

"That man is in several of them," said the librarian.

"Do you have dates for these pictures?" asked Jacob.

"Unfortunately we do not," answered the librarian. "Most of these pictures were recently donated by a former local resident."

"Maybe I can speak with that person," said Jacob.

"Not easily," said the librarian. "The pictures were donated as per their will."

"Oh," said Jacob. He continued to leaf through the pictures. Most were pictures of the downtown area, with several pictures of the building he occupied. The shop was a bakery in every picture. The businesses on either side changed from time to time.

"There was a lot of turnover on that street," explained the librarian. "Several businesses failed over time."

"But the bakery was always there," said Jacob.

"That's correct," said the librarian. "I don't always remember the shop open, but the building's always been a bakery."

"And you don't have any information on the owner?" asked Jacob.

"Unfortunately no," replied the librarian. "You will appear as the first recorded owner in several years."

"Can I get a copy of these pictures?" asked Jacob. "Maybe I can put some up in the shop."

"I'm sorry," said the librarian. "I can't allow the pictures to leave the library and we don't have a copier or scanner. I've asked the town council several times but they never seem to have the money."

"Maybe I can get the merchants to chip in," suggested Jacob.

"That would be welcome," said the librarian.

"Will you keep looking for more information?" asked Jacob.

"If you'd like," said the librarian.

"Thank you," replied Jacob.

"Stop back again," called the librarian as Jacob left the building.

Outside the library Jacob ran into Marlow. "Good afternoon, Jacob," said Marlow.

"Hello," replied Jacob. "Going to your daily reading?"

"Yes," confirmed Marlow. "I assume you were checking on the librarian's research on the bakery."

"He didn't find much," said Jacob. "Just some pictures. One I've already seen."

Marlow nodded. "Too few people take care to remember the past anymore," he said.

"I wish I knew more about the baker," said Jacob.

"Do you remember my story about the candles?" asked Marlow.

"Of course," said Jacob. "We were all pleasantly surprised at your participation in the fair."

"Everyone's total lack of faith in me aside," continued Marlow, "we never failed to light that candle while my father was away."

"I don't doubt it," said Jacob.

"Jacob, do you think my father would fail to come home if we did not light the candle?" asked Marlow.

"Probably not," said Jacob. "But it's a good tradition."

"I always knew it didn't matter," said Marlow. "But do you know why I never stopped lighting the candle?"

"Because of tradition," suggested Jacob.

"No," replied Marlow. "I never wanted to see for sure whether or not it would make a difference."

"I'm not sure I understand your point here," said Jacob.

"My point is," replied Marlow, "that some things are best undiscovered."

"You're referring to the baker," said Jacob.

"The man you know as the baker has obviously given you a great gift," said Marlow. "Why analyze it?"

"I want to know more about the man who helped me," said Jacob.

"He is the man who taught you a new trade," corrected Marlow. "Some things are best undiscovered."

"Are you implying that I'm going to find something bad?" asked Jacob.

"Not at all," replied Marlow. "Only that sometimes not knowing is better. That is one of the flaws in our society. We want to know everything. We have given up the unknown."

"I guess people want the reality," said Jacob.

"Sometimes the magical is the reality," said Marlow. He smiled and went into the library before Jacob had a chance to reply. Jacob realized it was the first time he'd seen Marlow smile.

30.

The first weekend of craft booths had gone less than perfect - almost all the crafters had left a mess. Jacob had spent most of the evening after closing sweeping and cleaning vacant stores. He returned to the bakery exhausted. The amount of the mess seemed disproportionate to the small size of the crowds.

"If only we'd gotten some news coverage," said Jacob out loud.

"Excuse me?" asked a man in a trim blue suit.

"I'm sorry," said Jacob. "I was just talking to myself. We're actually closed for the day. I don't have anything fresh."

"My fault," said the man in the blue suit. "I saw the light on and I just stopped in to talk to the owner."

"I'm not doing anymore interviews," said Jacob flatly.

"I'm not a reporter," clarified the man. He handed Jacob a business card. The man worked for a well-known food company. "You have a good thing going here."

"Thanks," said Jacob. "But what can I do for you?"

"Have you thought of franchising?" asked the man.

"You mean the bakery?" said Jacob gesturing at the walls around them.

"Yes," answered the man. "Or you could license the gingerbread men. My company is always looking for innovative products."

"I appreciate the offer," replied Jacob, "but it seems premature. I haven't been in business all that long. I've been working on the gingerbread men even less."

"I know it seems a little fast," said the man, "but you should capitalize on your recent exposure and expand now."

"I don't know," hesitated Jacob. "I'm happy with the way things are now."

"The increase in business won't last," cautioned the man.

"I'm sure it won't," said Jacob. "I was doing fine before the news story."

"Franchising or licensing can stabilize your business," said the man. "It can give you financial security."

This gave Jacob pause. His parents had always impressed him with the need for security. It was part of the reason he'd gone into his original career and part of the reason he'd been so nervous about leaving it. Was it possible to achieve the same security with the bakery?

Jacob was doing well but his daily income did differ day to day. There was no guarantee he'd continue to sell the gingerbread men or anything else for that matter. The bakery might just be a fad. A chain store bakery might open up on the highway.

"Take some time to think about it," said the man. "If you're interested in hearing more give me a call."

"Okay," said Jacob.

Jacob was actually too tired to give it much thought that night. He fell asleep not long after returning home and awoke wondering if the librarian had discovered any new information. It hadn't been many days since his last inquiry. Marlow's words had also left him unsure about things.

Jacob put the business of the baker's identity aside for the moment and thought about the man in the blue suit's suggestion. He liked the idea of his gingerbread men selling in other bakeries. However, he also liked the idea of being part of this town. Could he have both?

Income from franchising might give him more time with Kate. Often he and Kate were involved in activities for the shop. They filled orders or totaled receipts together. She seemed to enjoy the work but Jacob wished he could offer her more.

By lunchtime Jacob decided to call the man in the blue suit and at least listen to his proposal. The man suggested they meet for dinner. The man in the blue suit brought along several other men and women in blue suits from the food company. They explained to Jacob how they looked for products from restaurants and bakeries in small towns.

"We think it's important to maintain the integrity of the people and products we make part of our family," said the man in the blue suit.

By the time they got to dessert and coffee the man in the blue suit began to ask Jacob if he was ready to get started. Jacob pointed out they hadn't told him anything about the program itself. Jacob also wanted to talk to some of the other franchisees.

"Absolutely," answered the man in the blue suit. "I knew you were a smart man. I'll get you a list of people you can talk to."

"And I'd still like to hear more specifics about the program," added Jacob.

"I understand," said the man in the blue suit. "We'll come by the bakery tomorrow to tell you more."

The next day the man in the blue suit provided Jacob with a list of three names. Jacob called each name on the list. Each had a slightly different story but the message was the same. They echoed the sentiment of the men and women from the company. Each spoke about the exotic pursuits, hobbies or objects they were able to purchase as a result of the program.

The following day the man in the blue suit returned with one other colleague. As promised they outlined most of the specifics of the program. In Jacob's case the company felt it was best to simply license the custom gingerbread men.

Other bakeries would pay an upfront fee and commission on each cookie. In return they would receive Jacob's recipe for the three-season gingerbread and templates for creating the various decorations. All the designs would originate with Jacob and the company would enforce consistency among all the various bakeries.

Jacob would have to describe how he made and decorated the cookies to ensure consistency at other bakeries. The company would provide him with a space to work. Luckily the company headquarters was not far from the town. They suggested Jacob bake in the morning and hire someone to take his place in the afternoon.

The man in the blue suit was excited about Jacob's gingerbread men and suggested he start working on the standards and process documents right away. He could fill them out while the company was still finalizing the licensing agreements and designing the marketing campaigns.

"Then we can have Jacob attend some of the creative meetings," suggested the colleague of the man in the blue suit.

"Good idea," said the man. "We can also help you hire help for the afternoons."

Jacob rubbed his chin and looked at the papers before him. The smell of three-season gingerbread hung in the air. Several undecorated cookies were cooling nearby on the counter. A few completed orders waited to be picked up.

A familiar question arose in his mind. What's the worst that could happen? People might not buy the cookies outside of his bakery. The popularity of the gingerbread men could fade. He might not make as much as the company was promising. He was sure none of these things could cause him to lose the bakery.

Then another thought occurred to him. "Does the company own my recipe and designs?" asked Jacob.

"Not at all," answered the man in the blue suit. "We only get the right to distribute the recipe and design. In exchange we'll get a percentage of the fees and commissions. You own all your ideas."

"Even if the licensing program flops," said Jacob, "I still get to continue making the gingerbread men in my own bakery."

"I don't think that will happen," said the man in the blue suit, "but in the event it does you'll simply go back to baking in your own shop. You don't really have anything to lose."

"And potentially lots to gain," added the woman.

31.

"I don't know, Jacob," said Kate. "It all seems too good to be true."

"I don't think it will be as successful as they say," said Jacob. "But I don't see what it could hurt."

"Are you sure there's nothing to lose?" asked Kate.

"No," said Jacob. "I still own all my ideas. If it doesn't work I just keep working at the bakery. But if it works we'll have more time for each other."

"I notice you keep using the word 'we,'" pointed out Kate.

"Is it okay to use that word?" asked Jacob.

"You can use it," said Kate. She put her arms around him and kissed him.

They had dinner out for the first time in quite awhile. Jacob had worked extra hard during the afternoon to make sure all the orders were filled. Kate joked about the smell of gingerbread on his fingers.

"I'll need to document how the gingerbread men are created," said Jacob. "It's a lot of paperwork. I'll need to hire someone to work in the bakery during the afternoon."

"Hiring your first employee is a big milestone," said Kate.

"I know," said Jacob. "I'm not sure where to start. Should I just put an ad in the newspaper?"

"I think you should talk to the other storeowners first," suggested Kate. "Maybe they can recommend someone. Marlene goes through a lot of girls at the flower shop. She has a lot of experience hiring people."

"That's a good idea," said Jacob.

The next day Jacob got the opinion of the other shopkeepers on the plan. He started with Marlene since Kate thought she could be the most help. As usual he took a treat from the bakery with him.

"Always bearing gifts," said Marlene.

"Your flowers always brighten up the bakery," said Jacob. "I just like to return the favor."

"It is appreciated," said Marlene. "Now, Kate mentioned you were thinking of hiring someone for the afternoons."

"Yes," said Jacob. "Did she tell you about the licensing?"

"She did mention something," said Marlene. "But she said you could explain it better."

"I'm thinking about licensing the gingerbread men out to other bakeries," explained Jacob. "It would all be run through a major food company. They would handle the licensing and forward the commissions to me."

"Sounds like you're moving up," said Marlene.

"We'll see how it goes," said Jacob. "But I'll need someone to work the afternoon shift while I'm at the office."

"And Kate suggested you talk to me," said Marlene.

"She said you've done a lot of hiring," replied Jacob.

"I certainly have," said Marlene. "I've become a fairly good judge of character but I do make some mistakes."

"Probably less than I would make," said Jacob.

"Well," continued Marlene, "if you trust me I could find someone for you."

"I definitely trust your judgment," said Jacob. "I wouldn't know the first thing about hiring someone."

"I'll help you out this time," said Marlene, "since it sounds like you'll be busy. But next time its better if I show you how to hire. Teach a man to fish and all that."

"It's a deal," said. Jacob.

Jacob went on to visit the other merchants. He wanted their opinions on the licensing deal. The reactions were predictable. Chapal thought it was an excellent idea and Jacob was a lucky man to receive such an opportunity so early in the life of his business. Carson was worried about the whole thing although he couldn't exactly explain why.

The Moores thought he was selling out to something they called the "establishment." They couldn't completely explain what the establishment was or who might be a member of it. Jacob politely thanked them and moved on to Sofia, who wanted to know who booked the food company's travel. Jacob said he would try and find out.

As he worked his way through the neighborhood Jacob began to realize it was Marlow's opinion that interested him the most. Marlow may be difficult and pessimistic but he did have the oldest business in town. He had survived enough ups and downs over the years.

Marlow listened intently as Jacob explained the terms of the deal. He also asked more questions than any of the other shop owners. When Jacob was finished Marlow sat quiet for several minutes. He appeared to be deep in thought. Finally he looked back at Jacob.

"Financially it's a good deal," concluded Marlow. "If it works you can make a lot of money. If it doesn't you still have the business."

"You think so?" asked Jacob.

"The biggest pitfall is that if this company is not successful marketing your product you'll be unable to offer the product to another one," said Marlow.

"I didn't think about that," said Jacob.

"There is something else," continued Marlow. "If it is successful, have you thought about what it might mean for you and the bakery?"

"More exposure I would think," said Jacob.

"It means less baking," said Marlow. "You already have to cut back on your hours to get things started. Is that something you want to do?"

"That's just for a short time," said Jacob.

"Perhaps," replied Marlow.

They sat quietly for a few moments. Jacob thought about what Marlow said. He decided Marlow was assuming the worst as usual. He was more interested in Marlow's financial advice anyway. He had built up a successful business, not necessarily a happy one. Jacob shifted the conversation back to the business side of the deal.

"Would you trust the company?" asked Jacob.

"From what I've heard, the company you're speaking with is reputable," answered Marlow. "They've brought out several successful products like yours."

"Would you take the deal?" asked Jacob.

"I can't answer that question, Jacob," said Marlow. "My business is much different than yours. Look around this store. All of this furniture was designed and built by other people."

"But you choose what to sell," said Jacob.

"Think about the inventory in your shop right now," said Marlow. "Everything in it was made by you, was it not?"

"I guess it was," said Jacob.

"Of course it was," said Marlow, "everything you sell was created by you. The food company will be selling a piece of you. Only you can decide whether or not you can live with that."

"You've given me a lot to think about," said Jacob.

"That was the idea," replied Marlow. He looked at his watch. "I believe your afternoon rush will be starting soon."

"Yes," said Jacob. He went back to the bakery.

After closing for the day Jacob called the man in the blue suit. Jacob asked how soon he'd have to decide whether or not to take the deal. The man explained the company wanted to do some additional market studies first. In the meantime the man in the blue suit suggested Jacob start coming into the office to document his standards and practices.

Jacob thought that was reasonable. He told the man in the blue suit he would start coming in as soon as he hired help for the afternoon rush. The man asked if he needed assistance. Jacob said no. After saying goodbye Jacob ended the call and locked up for the night.

32.

Jacob lifted his hands off the keyboard and cracked his knuckles. His mother had always taught him it was a terrible habit, but it felt good. He sat back in his chair and looked at the screen. Jacob had been working at the food company office in the afternoons for over a week. Earlier that day the man in the blue suit had suggested Jacob start coming in all day.

Jacob said he would consider it but offered a half-hearted excuse about the orderliness of the shop. In truth the bakery was actually cleaner than he usually left it. Marlene had picked well.

Sandy, his new afternoon help, had worked in the flower shop for almost six months before coming to the bakery. Marlene explained she was a very hard worker but didn't really like the flower shop. Jacob suspected Marlene had Sandy in mind from the moment he asked for help. Sandy told Jacob she enjoyed working in the bakery much more than the flower shop. Jacob also noticed he tended to sell more in the afternoons with Sandy on the register.

Jacob put his hands back down on the keys and continued to type. He got through a few sentences before noticing he wasn't really saying anything. Jacob looked at his watch. It was just after four, about the time the first of the evening trains arrived. Three people always came into the bakery from that train.

The first was a tall woman who always wore a trim pantsuit. The woman would carefully examine several round rolls before choosing the one she considered the best. She always paid in cash and always explained to Jacob that she'd be eating the roll with a large salad.

The second was a large man who was always in a hurry. He never seemed to buy the same thing twice but he always chose what to buy quickly. The man was in and out of the bakery within a couple of minutes. He regularly allowed Jacob to keep any change from the purchase. This enabled the large man to simply set a few bills on the counter and leave.

The third was a short, quiet man who bought six long rolls each workday and a cake or pie on Friday. The man wore a wedding band so Jacob assumed the man had a family. He imagined the man had four children based on the six rolls he always bought. It occurred to Jacob the man could have five children assuming he or his wife did not eat a roll.

"Jacob?" said a voice behind him. "Jacob, you're late."

Jacob turned around in his chair to find a colleague of the man in the blue suit standing behind him. "Late?" he asked.

"Yes," said the woman. "There was a market survey meeting planned for four o'clock. You're already ten minutes late."

"I'm sorry," said Jacob.

"That's okay," replied the woman. "They probably started without you."

Jacob got up and started to walk down the hall to his right.

"Jacob," the woman called after him. "The conference room is in the other direction."

"Sorry," said Jacob again. He walked down the hallway the other direction. This time the woman led the way. They entered a large room where several people in suits were already seated around a long table. Jacob looked down at the t-shirt and jeans he was wearing. He felt completely out of place as the woman shepherded him to a seat.

Several of the people at the table glanced briefly at Jacob and then returned their attention to a woman standing and speaking at the other end of the table. Jacob felt like he'd just walked into the middle of a college lecture the day before a mid-term.

Someone passed a report binder over to Jacob and he paged through it. It contained several pages of text, each with plenty of footnotes. Only the occasional graph or table broke up the long paragraphs. Jacob couldn't tell what any of it had to do with baking. He tried reading the first couple of pages but that only made him more confused.

Jacob looked around the room at the other people seated at the table. Among them he only recognized the man in the blue suit who had originally visited him and the woman who had escorted him to the meeting. He had never seen any of the other people before, including the woman making the presentation.

Jacob tried to get the man in the blue suit's attention. He began by whispering. At first the man in the blue suit didn't appear to notice. He seemed engrossed in the woman's presentation. Jacob reached over and tapped the man on the forearm. Another man next to Jacob gave him an annoyed look.

Jacob tapped the man in the blue suit on the forearm again. This time the man gave Jacob a confused look. He made a gesture with his hands as if to ask Jacob "What is the matter?"

"What's the meeting about?" whispered Jacob. The man in the blue suit reached over and pointed to the report binder. Jacob looked down at the report and frowned. "I don't understand this," he whispered.

The man in the blue suit reacted by placing his finger up to his lips. "But I don't know what's going on," protested Jacob. The man in the blue suit didn't answer. He went back to listening to the woman giving the presentation.

"Our projections show people prefer a more limited number of choices," said the woman. "Too many choices confuses them."

"That's a deviation from the full customization we've previously spoke about," said a man at the table.

"Yes," answered the woman. "But we believe it is warranted given the market research in this area. Several focus groups reacted negatively when faced with an open-ended choice. Scores were much better when groups were presented with a number of closed-ended choices."

"What if their choice isn't represented?" asked another woman at the table.

"Research from similar product areas indicate people will simply chose the closest variation," replied the presenter.

Jacob moved his head back and forth to each person as they spoke, as if looking directly at them would give him a better understanding of the conversation. He began to consider the possibility he'd been pulled into the wrong meeting. This certainly didn't sound like a presentation about gingerbread cookies.

"Several of the variations are similar," pointed out the man in the blue suit. "People tend to see what they want to see."

"That's correct," confirmed the woman presenter. "People will naturally gravitate towards the most relevant variation. We recommend a core base of fifteen variations. This also allows us to standardized pricing."

"We can charge extra for orders outside of the core," suggested a different man at the table.

"Excellent idea," agreed the man in the blue suit.

"How do we choose the core variations?" asked the woman who had escorted Jacob to the meeting.

"We're conducting research on the most common professions," replied the woman presenter. "We're cross checking against professions requiring similar garments in order to maximize coverage within the core."

Several men and women at the table nodded with approval. The mention of the word "profession" stuck in Jacob's mind. He finally understood the purpose of the meeting.

"I don't limit the number of jobs," he interjected. Several of the people at the table turned to look at him with puzzled looks on their faces.

"I'll create whatever job a customer asks for," continued Jacob. "That's the idea of the gingerbread men."

"Who is this man?" asked someone at the table.

"I thought he was a corporate messenger," said another.

"This is Jacob," explained the man in the blue suit. "He is the baker who created the three season gingerbread and the custom gingerbread men."

The room was quiet for a few moments. During that time several of the men and women at the table looked at Jacob. Some took notes on their pads. Others looked away or whispered to their neighbors. Jacob looked at the man in the blue suit for guidance. The man was scribbling something on his own pad.

Finally a man at the other end of the table spoke. "Does he need to be here?" he asked.

33.

Jacob decided to skip the office the next day. The meeting left him with a headache. The only way he could get rid of it was to go back to the bakery and make several batches of cookies and a pie. The next morning he called the man in the blue suit and told him things were too busy at the shop for him to come in that day.

The man in the blue suit did not seem concerned. He told Jacob the meeting had gone well and all the research looked positive. The food company was about ready to move forward with his agreement. He said Jacob would probably receive all the paperwork to sign sometime the following week.

Jacob was happy to get back to the bakery. The morning was especially busy. The trains were running late so commuters had little to do but eat muffins and drink coffee. Several even lingered in the shop longer than usual. This gave Jacob to the opportunity to talk with several of the customers.

Jacob was disappointed when the trains began to catch up and the morning commuters drifted off to work. He decided to spend more time talking with the customers in the future. He wanted to learn the stories behind all of those windows in town.

Jacob had an early lunch with Kate before starting his afternoon baking. He told her about his confusion at the previous day's meeting. She laughed when he explained the meeting was actually about the choices of gingerbread men.

"Jacob," said Kate after she finished laughing, "You know I support whatever decision you make. But is this really what you want?"

"What do you mean?" asked Jacob.

"I understand the benefits," continued Kate. "But is it worth all this?"

"It's not that bad," said Jacob.

"We're laughing about it now," said Kate. "But how did you feel yesterday?"

"Like I was back in college and late for my exams," replied Jacob.

"Exactly," said Kate. "You don't fit in with these people."

Jacob thought about this. He was undeniably out of place at the meeting. However, he had to admit he hadn't been reading most of the documents the man in the blue suit had been sending him. Several were piled in his living room. Jacob recalled the report on top of the pile had several drink stains on it.

"Maybe I just need to prepare better," said Jacob. "I haven't been reading anything about the project."

"You mean those documents on the coffee table?" asked Kate. "They seemed like a bunch of gibberish to me."

"You just have to speak their language," replied Jacob.

"And you do?" countered Kate.

"A little," said Jacob.

They finished lunch and Jacob went back to work at the bakery. He finished up the day's gingerbread orders and prepared for the afternoon rush. He had given Sandy the day off. Jacob had told her it was a well-deserved break but in reality he was looking forward to handling the bakery on his own.

That afternoon Jacob custom decorated forty-two different gingerbread men. He noted how much faster he had gotten at the task. He also thought his designs had improved. He broadened the edible items he used for decoration and gave the gingerbread men a more three-dimensional look.

As he completed the last cookie Jacob thought about the "core" mentioned at the meeting. He understood the report enough to know the food company was considering a total of only fifteen to twenty designs. Jacob looked down at the over forty cookies he had decorated. He tried to imagine completing the orders with only twenty different designs.

"I can make it better," said Jacob out loud. "That's why the company has me come in every day, so I can help them do it right."

"Who are you trying to convince?" asked Ted. He'd come into the bakery as Jacob was staring at the gingerbread men.

Jacob turned around with a start. "Oh, it's you, Ted," he said.

"Didn't mean to startle you," said Ted. "I hope you weren't talking to the cookies."

"No," said Jacob. "Not yet."

"Stressed over the big deal?" asked Ted.

"I suppose so," replied Jacob. "I had a long day yesterday."

"Wouldn't catch me at one of those places," said Ted. "I don't even like doing paperwork at the end my shift."

"Does any policeman like doing paperwork?" asked Jacob.

"I guess not," replied Ted. "I'm sure you'll figure it all out. Didn't you used to work for a company like this before the bakery?"

"Yes," said Jacob. "Coffee?"

"Definitely," answered Ted. "That's actually why I came in. Let me get a roll and some butter too."

"You got it," said Jacob. "I have some time before the next rush. Care to stay and chat?"

Ted checked with his dispatch and nodded. The two sat down and Jacob also had a cup of coffee and a roll. He left off the butter, though. Jacob was a bit worried about his weight now that he was spending more time behind a desk.

They chatted about the bakery and about the deal. Jacob told Ted about the meeting and had him laughing even more than Kate. Jacob tended to embellish and exaggerate the story a bit more each time he told it. The latest version had him tugging on the man in the blue suit's sleeve and several people dozing off during the presentation.

Ted left shortly before the first few customers arrived. Jacob greeted each of the evening commuters with genuine enthusiasm. He was happy to see each one, even the grumpier ones. Jacob discovered if he was consistently cheery they were often in a better mood by the time they left the bakery.

Jacob recognized his regulars the same way he had in the morning and he discovered he missed them all. He spoke to them more than usual. The conversations were bittersweet – Jacob kept remembering he'd have to go back to the company the next day.

Jacob kept the bakery open later than usual. He didn't have many customers once the usual evening crowds waned. However, a few stragglers were happy to find the bakery still open. Most asked if he was going to extend the hours. Jacob told them he was considering it.

After the last customer left, Jacob lingered over the end of day cleanup. He picked up the items to be packed away one at a time and wiped the counters more slowly than usual. Jacob continued to sweep and mop long after the floors were clean.

"Are you trying to take the finish off the floors?" asked Kate as she walked into the kitchen. Jacob didn't see her come in and jumped at the sound of her voice. "Sorry, I didn't mean to scare you," she said.

"You're not the first person to startle me today," said Jacob.

"You seem to be deep in thought today," replied Kate.

"Just appreciating the day," said Jacob.

"As opposed to yesterday?" asked Kate.

"I've been thinking," answered Jacob. "I just need to be more active at the food company. Starting tomorrow I'm going to participate more. I can improve things."

"Who are you trying to convince?" asked Kate.

34.

Jacob used the following evening to read through the most recent reports from the food company. By the time he went into the office he felt much more confident about the project. Instead of going directly to his desk he went to the office of the man in the blue suit.

The man in the blue suit was very excited to see him. Once inside the office he sat Jacob down in a soft leather chair opposite his desk. The man sat down behind the desk and passed several large pieces of cardboard over to Jacob. "Take a look at these," said the man triumphantly.

"What are these?" asked Jacob as he leafed through the pieces of cardboard. Each contained a small sketch on a white piece of paper.

"Sketches of the advertising campaign for the gingerbread men, of course," replied the man.

"Oh," said Jacob. He looked through the sketches. "These don't actually have any gingerbread men on them."

"Yes," said the man in the blue suit. "That's the genius of the campaign."

Jacob was beginning to have that feeling of being late for a mid-term again. "I don't think I understand," he said. "How can we sell gingerbread men without showing the cookies?"

"Just leave that to us," replied the man in the blue suit. The man shuffled some papers around his desk. He looked up to see Jacob still staring at the drawings. "How are you coming with the standards and process documents?"

"Okay," said Jacob. He put down the cardboard pages. "I wanted to talk to you about the choices of gingerbread men."

"You mean the core?" asked the man.

'That's right," replied Jacob.

"Excellent idea, isn't it?" said the man.

"Actually," began Jacob. "I don't think we should limit the number of choices. I was able to decorate over forty different designs yesterday. Each one of the designs was a custom order. No one seemed confused by too many choices."

The man in the blue suit held up his hand. "Jacob, I want to hear all about it," he said.

Jacob smiled. He knew he could make a difference by speaking up. After he convinced the company about the gingerbread choices he'd get back to the advertising campaign. Jacob didn't know a lot about advertising but was sure you couldn't sell rolls and cookies without actually showing them.

"As soon as I finish returning some phone calls," said the man in the blue suit.

Jacob's attention turned back to the man. "Excuse me?" asked Jacob.

"I want to hear all about your ideas as soon as I finish making some phone calls," said the man in the blue suit.

"Oh," said Jacob.

"I'll have my assistant let you know when I'm finished," said the man. He signaled to his assistant who entered the room and led Jacob out. Before he could say another word Jacob found himself back in the hallway.

"I'll come get you at your desk when he's ready," said the assistant.

"I think I'll wait," said Jacob. He sat down on a chair outside of the office and folded his hands. "I'm sure he won't be too long."

The assistant got up and said something through the door to the office. After a moment she nodded and turned back to Jacob. "That will be fine," she said.

Jacob sat back in the chair and waited. In the background he could hear the man in the blue suit talking on the phone. The man made several calls. Each time he hung up, Jacob rose slightly in his chair. Then he would hear the man speak a greeting and start another conversation. This went on throughout the afternoon.

Eventually Jacob lost track of time and stopped rising in his chair at each break in the conversation. He looked up at the clock on the wall. Jacob couldn't remember what time he'd arrived at the office but it seemed like a long time since he'd looked at the drawings.

Jacob experienced another bit of hope when the assistant stood up a short time later. She picked up several pieces of paper and appeared to be walking right towards Jacob. He started to get up again but she passed by him without a word. Jacob watched her go over to a machine in the corner.

The assistant dropped the paper into the machine and pressed a button. A series of slicing sounds came from the machine and the papers came out the other side in thin crinkly strips. Jacob watched the assistant repeat this several more times. He was grateful for the distraction.

After the assistant finished shredding papers, Jacob passed the time by watching a shadow from the window work it's way across the floor. As it moved further to the right the light outside changed from a bright white to a dull orange. Jacob was starting to drift off to sleep when the man in the blue suit finally exited his office.

"Jacob," said the man in the blue suit, "you're still here. I thought you'd gone back to your desk."

"I didn't realize it would be so long," said Jacob. "I was sure you'd come out at any minute."

"I kept meaning to," replied the man, "but the work just keeps piling up sometimes. "

"Can we talk now?" asked Jacob.

"There's nothing I'd like more," said the man. Jacob started to get up from his chair. "I just can't right now. My wife is expecting me home for dinner."

"Right," said Jacob.

"We'll talk tomorrow," said the man in the blue suit as he hurried down the hallway.

"Today's Friday," pointed out Jacob.

"So it is," said the man turning around briefly. "We'll have lots to talk about on Monday then. One of the people I spoke with today was the head of our legal division. All your contracts should be ready for you to sign next week."

Jacob watched the man go down the hallway. "I'd like to schedule an appointment for Monday afternoon," he said turning back to the assistant. Jacob found himself facing an empty chair and desk. Apparently the assistant had left as well.

Jacob left the food company's building and went to the train station. He had missed his usual train so Jacob sat down to wait again. The train arrived and Jacob drifted into the last car.

He slumped down in an empty seat and watched the lights go by without focusing as the train traveled from the city to the town.

35.

Saturday was Jacob's favorite day of the week. Everyone was happier on Saturday. Many were not in as much of a hurry. More and more customers were also staying to eat at the tables outside the bakery. Even the foods they bought were more festive. During the week Jacob sold mostly rolls and bagels. On Saturdays he sold mostly cakes, pies and cookies.

Kate usually hung around the shop on Saturdays as well. She spent a good portion of the time waiting on customers and clearing the outside tables. Kate managed to have at least a brief conversation with almost everyone. Many people she already knew from her work with the fire department.

Jacob admired the way Kate was able to remember everyone's name. He was only good at remembering faces and occupations – especially if they had ordered a gingerbread man. Jacob liked to picture the person in their job as he decorated their cookie.

"The couple outside wants another round of pie," said Kate coming back into the bakery. "If you dish it up I'll take it out."

"Just let me finish off these customers," replied Jacob. "In the meantime, can you get a coffee and a blueberry muffin ready for Marlene? She should be here in a few minutes."

"I think Carson's coming in too," said Kate.

"Who's minding the shoe store?" asked Jacob.

"Chapal's niece is working there now," said Kate.

"When did that happen?" asked Jacob as he wrapped up a dozen cookies for a waiting customer. He closed out the sale and started slicing the pie for the customers outside.

"Last week," answered Kate.

"Oh," said Jacob. He handed Kate the pie. "I guess I missed it." Kate gave him a peck on the cheek and took out the order. Jacob smiled as he watched her leave the shop. As she was serving the pie, Marlene arrived and gave her a hug. Jacob poured another cup of coffee for Kate and placed it on the table where Marlene's coffee and muffin were already waiting.

Marlene and Kate reentered and went to their table. Jacob went over and started to talk to them but several more customers entered the bakery. "Better get back to the counter," he said.

"You should see if Sandy can take some Saturday hours," said Marlene. "You could use an extra person at the counter."

"Good idea," replied Jacob as he began to fill the current orders. While he was working Carson and Chapal came into the shop. They joined Kate and Marlene. Kate spoke to them for a moment and came over to the counter.

"Plain bagel and a jelly donut," said Kate. "I'll get it. Finish out these customers."

"Thanks," said Jacob. "Hail, hail the gang's all here."

"Just about," replied Kate. "We're missing Ted and Sofia"

"Ted was in this morning," said Jacob. "Sofia is watching her figure."

"No coffee?" asked Kate putting the bagel and donut on plates.

"Carson is also avoiding caffeine," replied Jacob.

"See," said Kate, "you haven't missed everything."

"Not yet," replied Jacob. He finished off the last few customers and was able to join the others for some late breakfast.

Marlene, Carson and Chapal had to return to their respective shops but Kate stayed on throughout the afternoon. Marlow entered the shop as they were cleaning up and packaging gingerbread orders.

"Can I speak with you a moment?" asked Marlow.

"Definitely," replied Jacob.

"Alone," said Marlow flatly.

"I'll wrap up the extra dough in the kitchen," said Kate.

"Thank you," said Marlow.

"Good to see you too, Marlow," said Kate as she left the room.

"What's going on?" asked Jacob.

"Please extend my apologies to the young lady," said Marlow. "But I prefer to keep my business private."

"I understand," replied Jacob. He actually had no idea why Marlow had come for a visit much less asked Kate to leave the room.

As usual, Marlow came right to the point. "Jacob, I've decided to retire," he said.

Jacob was speechless. He had never imagined the furniture store or the town without Marlow glooming about. "What will you do?" he asked.

"I'm going south to live with my brother," replied Marlow. "I've sold furniture since I was fourteen. That's long enough for any man."

"I'll miss you," said Jacob. It came out as instinctual politeness but Jacob realized he actually meant it. "I mean that," he added.

"Surprised yourself a bit there," observed Marlow. Jacob almost thought he saw a smile on Marlow's lips. If it was there it only stayed for an instant.

"When are you leaving?" asked Jacob.

"Tonight," said Marlow. "I've already put things in order with the store. It will be sold in my absence. Try to make sure it's bought by another family."

"I will," said Jacob. "But why leave so quickly?"

"To avoid the gaudy send off you and the others would have cooked up," answered Marlow. "I'll trust you to convey my goodbyes to everyone."

Jacob nodded. "I know they'll be sorry they missed you," he said.

"I doubt that," said Marlow. "Nonetheless, I also wanted to give you something."

Marlow reached into his coat and took out a thickly stuffed envelope and handed it to Jacob. "In that envelope are the answers you seek," he said. Marlow gestured at the ivy carvings in the bakery's shelves.

"But how?" started Jacob.

"We take furniture in trade," replied Marlow. "Sometimes even from town hall. Items and papers are often left inside. I've amassed quite a collection of documents over the years."

"Why keep it?" asked Jacob.

"I believe the librarian already told you about the fire," said Marlow. "I thought it more prudent to keep the records in my own safe. Now that I'm retiring I'm turning all the documents back to the town. The ones in this envelope relate to the baker."

"The librarian will be disappointed he wasn't the one to find them," said Jacob.

"I wanted you to have them directly," said Marlow, "because you must make your own choice regarding them."

"I don't understand," said Jacob. "Is there something bad in here?"

"You're missing my point," said Marlow. "The choice is whether or not to look at the documents in the first place. I could have tried not lighting the candles just to see if my father would still come home. Do you want the reality or do you want the magic?"

Jacob looked down at the envelope. He was unsure whether he wanted to open it or not. He looked back at Marlow for guidance.

"Sometimes the mystery is better," said Marlow. This time Jacob was sure he saw a smile on his lips. Without another word Marlow turned and left the bakery.

36.

When Jacob arrived at the food company that Monday a business contract was on his desk, just as the man in the blue suit had promised. He stared at the first page, which was densely covered with writing. Jacob flipped through the pages. Each piled on paragraph after paragraph of tightly packed words.

Jacob pushed the contract aside and set the envelope he'd gotten from Marlow on his desk. He still had not decided whether or not to open it. He wanted to know more about the baker but he also didn't want to lose the magic as Marlow had pointed out.

What's the worst that could happen? There would be nothing special in the envelope. The baker could turn out to be an ordinary man. He could learn there was nothing special about the baker or the bakery. Jacob would no longer have anything to wonder about.

In this case Jacob realized he could not live with the worst. He thought back to the first day he'd met the baker. Jacob remembered seeing the baker sweeping out in front of the store. He remembered the day the baker taught him about high protein and low protein dough. Jacob decided he liked the mystery.

Jacob shoved the envelope aside and started reading through the food company contract again. He tried to concentrate on the words but kept thinking about the bakery. Right now he'd be taking fresh rolls out of the oven and placing them in bins. After that he'd put out the sweets such as pies, cakes and cookies.

Jacob forced his attention back to the contract. He was trying to read the section on which items were covered under the agreement. "Gingerbread flavored baked products with custom decorations" were about the only words on the page he could understand. Jacob always put the gingerbread cookies out last in the afternoon. The scent of ginger punctuated the other smells already present in the shop.

Jacob noted that those final few minutes before the evening rush arrived were some of the best in the bakery. The shop was fully stocked and everything was in its place. Jacob would always pause and enjoy the smells drifting up from the displays.

"I see you received the contract," said a voice behind him. Jacob turned around to find the man in the blue suit.

"Yes," said Jacob.

"Good," said the man. He handed Jacob another set of papers. "Here are some projections for the first six months. I think we're both going to be very happy with this arrangement."

Jacob didn't reply. "Let me know if you have any questions," said the man in the blue suit.

"Actually," replied Jacob, "I do have some questions about the contract."

"Of course," said the man. "I just need to get these projections into a report and then we can talk about it. I'll have my assistant call when I'm finished." The man in the blue suit started to walk away then paused and turned back to face Jacob. "No need to wait in the area outside my office," he said.

Jacob watched him walk away and went back to the contract. He tried reading but couldn't concentrate. A dust of white powder near his red company coffee mug drew his attention. Jacob realized it was powdered creamer. He stared at the powder and wondered if he could use powdered milk to hold his homemade breakfast bars together.

Jacob brushed the powder off his fingers and went back to reading the report. He couldn't remember where he'd left off so he had to start from the beginning. All he could think about was trying to bake a new batch of breakfast bars. He set the document back down and stared blankly forward.

Jacob looked at his surroundings and felt his heart sink, pressing on his diaphragm. He winced to avoid a scream. The company mug might be red instead of green but it was all the same as before.

"What's the worst that could happen?" He might never spend another afternoon at the bakery. No one here will listen to my ideas. They'll ruin my creations. They'll take away the magic. That was the worst that could happen.

Jacob pushed back on his chair and stood up. He picked up the red coffee mug and dropped it into the trash. Jacob grabbed the contract and the envelope Marlow had given him. He walked down the hall to the area outside of the man in blue suit's office.

"He can't see you right now," said the assistant as he walked up. "He's very busy."

Jacob didn't say a word. He walked past the assistant and over to the machine in the corner. Jacob dropped the contract in first. It came out the other side of the machine in a series of long strips. Next Jacob dropped in the envelope. The machine made a much deeper, slower sound than usual and appeared to struggle for a moment. The machine recovered and another set of strips came out of the other side.

Jacob smiled and walked away. By the time he got to the front doors of the building he was running. He ran until he reached the train. This time there was a train waiting when he arrived at the station. Jacob got into the first car but continued to move from one end of the train to the other as it made its way back to his home.

As soon as the doors opened Jacob bolted out and onto the station platform. He ran down the street to the bakery. For a moment he thought he saw the baker out front sweeping the stoop. As he got closer he realized it was Sandy. Jacob greeted her and ran inside the shop.

He looked at the clock and saw it wasn't yet time for the evening rush. Jacob went into the kitchen and put on his apron. The evening's tray of gingerbread men sat waiting on the counter. Jacob picked them up and carried them out into the front of the shop. He enjoyed the crisp smell of spice as he placed them one by one into the glass case.

While he was putting the last couple of cookies into the case Kate came into the bakery. "You're home early," she said.

"I am home," said Jacob.

"Did you sign the contract?" asked Kate.

"No," replied Jacob. "I ran."

"I don't understand," said Kate.

"I ran away," answered Jacob.

"You ran away from the food company," said Kate.

"I ran away from the fox," said Jacob.

Kate smiled. Jacob walked over and gave her a hug and a kiss. "I ran and ran," he said. "They can't catch me, because I'm the gingerbread man."

Three–season Gingerbread

Ingredients:

1 cup of margarine
1 cup of sugar
1 egg
1 cup of molasses
4 ½ cups of all-purpose flour
1 teaspoon of ground ginger
1 ½ teaspoons of baking soda
½ teaspoons of ground cloves
½ teaspoon of salt
1 teaspoon of vanilla
1 teaspoon of ground cinnamon

Steps:

1. In a mixing bowl combine margarine, molasses, egg, cinnamon and sugar. Mix until smooth and creamy. Add the dry ingredients and mix well. Refrigerate overnight.

2. Lightly flour a surface and roll out the dough to approximately 1/8th inch thickness.

3. Cut into desired shapes and place 1 inch apart on a lightly greased baking sheet. Bake at 350 degrees for 7 to 9 minutes.

Makes 5 to 6 dozen cookies.

Discussion Questions

1. How is Jacob like the gingerbread man in the classic children's poem? Does the poem inspire Jacob, or does he simply fulfill the prophesy of the verses?

2. Who is the baker? What does he represent?

3. How do the baker's principles relate to baking and life in general? In what ways does Jacob live the principles?

4. What is the significance of the different types of protein and the role of each in baking? How does this relate to life in general?

5. What does the glass display case represent to the baker? To Jacob?

6. Who are the "foxes" the baker refers to throughout the story? What do they represent?

7. What is the significance of people who are unnamed within the story, such as the man in the blue suit?

8. How do the custom gingerbread men relate to the "windows" and Jacob's curiosity about them?

9. What archetype characters do each of the merchants represent? What role does each play in the story?

10. How does the relationship between Jacob and Kate relate to his journey to become the baker?

11. What is Marlow's role in the story? How does he help Jacob transform his life?

12. How is Jacob similar to the baker? How is he different?

13. What challenges does Jacob face throughout the story and how does he overcome them?

14. Why does Jacob choose to destroy the information about the baker without looking at it?